ROBB WHITE is an authority on deep-sea adventure. In line of duty, as a Lt. Commander in the Navy, he has patrolled our island-studded southern waters. And just for fun, as a skilled small-boat skipper, he has explored many a sub-tropical bay and reef. No wonder his sailing yarns seem so real!

SECRET SEA

by

ROBB WHITE

illustrated by
RAY QUIGLEY

SCHOLASTIC BOOK SERVICES

Published by Scholastic Book Services, a division
of Scholastic Magazines, Inc., New York, N.Y.

6th printing........................July 1964

Printed in the U.S.A.

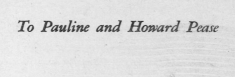

To Pauline and Howard Pease

Contents

THE FIRST BOOK

LOG OF THE "SANTA YBEL"

CHAPTER		PAGE
One	HEAVY WEATHER	3
Two	BEWARE THE TALL ONE	16
Three	TOP SECRET	32
Four	THE QUARTERBACK	44
Five	THE PURPLE HEART	62

THE SECOND BOOK

ESCAPE

One	MIKE	77
Two	BLOOD ON THE FACEPLATE	93
Three	THE BLACK SLOOP	108
Four	TRAPPED	124
Five	PHANTOM	140
Six	DINGHY ADRIFT	154

CONTENTS

THE THIRD BOOK

SECRET SEA

CHAPTER		PAGE
One	HIDEAWAY	171
Two	CONTACT	186
Three	CEPHALOPOD	205
Four	THE CONFLICT IS JOINED	219
Five	THE WHEEL OF YEARS	237
Six	MUTINY	254
Seven	SUGAR OPTION SUGAR	270
Eight	THE NOOSE DRAWS TIGHT	286
Nine	D DAY, H HOUR	306
Ten	NO BRIGHT RED BICYCLE	318

SECRET SEA

Book One

LOG OF THE "SANTA YBEL"

1

Heavy Weather

PETE MARTIN

Lieutenant Commander Pete Martin, USNR, commanding USS PC 237, watched his ship labor in the storm. Coming through the noise of wind and sea, he could hear the throbbing of the engines, hear the crying of metal ribs and backbone in his ship as the sea tried to take her apart. When her stern was lifted clear of the water, he could feel the beat of the screws going wild in nothing but air and he could imagine what the Black Gang was taking, trying to slow them before the brass wheels wrung themselves off the shafts. He watched a man open the door of the

3

deckhouse only to have a wave smash it shut again. It took the man three tries to get out the door.

On the open bridge Pete stood against the gun shield. As the waves came rushing up over the bow he, and all hands on the bridge, would duck and then rise slowly again to peer into the gray world ahead of the ship. Pete, feeling cold water inside his foul-weather gear, scowled, for he knew that it was wetting down the brand-new lieutenant commander shoulder boards he was wearing.

The executive officer, Lieutenant Randle, moved aft across the bridge. Sliding his hands along the top of the screen and sliding his feet so as never to have either feet or hands adrift, he got to the gun shield.

Cupping his hand around his mouth, he shouted, "Haven't you had enough of this, Captain?"

Pete watched the water running down Randle's face and into his mouth. He had a bitter, angry expression, and, during the short time Pete had been aboard as commanding officer, he had found Randle to be a poor officer and an unpleasant shipmate.

Pete shook his head and then pushed Randle down as a wave came roaring over the top of the screen.

When they were standing up again, Randle said, "I'm fed up with this weather, Captain."

The statement made Pete much angrier than it should have. But ever since he had reported aboard Randle had irritated him. Pete tried to remember that it wasn't Randle's fault if the Navy let him spend the years of the war sailing around Key West, Florida. But Pete had seen too much of the Pacific to remember things like that.

"Please continue Search Plan Baker, Mr. Randle," Pete said.

Randle shrugged. As he turned away he said, "Search plan! You couldn't find the U.S. Fleet in this weather."

Pete watched him go to the front of the bridge and stand staring out at the grayness, ducking when the waves came over.

What Randle had said began to worry Pete. Perhaps, he thought, this was too much weather for a green crew in a small ship. Perhaps he should give the order to turn and run for Key West. After all, Pete argued to himself, this is only training. This isn't for keeps the way it was out there. And it was certainly heavy going, with the screws thrashing in the air half the time, the bow down under green, the seas trying to carry away everything on deck that wasn't welded down.

Then Pete remembered the typhoon he had gone through off the Philippines in the destroyer *Hoel*. Compared to that, this was just a breeze of wind. Pete looked down at his ship. She was taking it all right. The engines were reacting nicely and the big sailor at the helm had lost his nervousness and was manhandling her through the seas, the spokes of the wheel throwing a whirl of water when he brought her up to meet the waves. It was, Pete decided, good training.

He relaxed against the gun shield and thought about the poor *Hoel*. Then, almost in amazement, he thought, I'm alive!

He remembered the way the Pacific looked on the morning of October 24, East Longitude Time. Not like the Gulf now—the water out there was a clear purple-blue, the gentle waves were sparkling, and the foam on them was as white as a little girl's Sunday dress. When the *Hoel* slid at thirty knots out from under the rain squall, it was like the lights going up in a movie. The Japanese battleships stood out clear and sharp against the sky, their cluttered masts like Christmas trees. When they fired the first salvo, they completely disappeared behind the blot of ugly yellow-black smoke.

Off to one side another destroyer, *Heerman*, was bucketing along, and the little destroyer escort, *Roberts*, was panting to keep up. Farther aft, the *Johnston* limped. Pete could see that she was badly hurt although he did not know then that every officer on her bridge had been killed or wounded when the battleship salvo hit her.

Already the escort carrier *Gambier Bay* had been slugged and was dead in the water. *Fanshaw*

6

Bay was a mess below decks but was still moving; *Kalinin Bay's* flight deck looked like Swiss cheese where the salvoes had gone clean through her. To save the rest of the jeep carriers, the three cans and the DE were going in. Four little ships against a Japanese battle fleet. Four little ships, one of them already mortally wounded.

The Japs turned everything they had on the four little ships. The battlewagons were using dye marker for the main batteries and, when the fourteen-inch shells struck the sea, tall waterspouts leaped up colored red or green or yellow or purple. The small stuff laced the blue water and the tracers shone yellow and cold in the sun.

The waterspouts were falling on the little ships as they settled down for the long torpedo run. Pete Martin glanced at a man crouching beside him and was surprised to find that it was his friend, Lieutenant (j.g.) Williams, for his face was streaked with red, green, and purple dye. Williams must have seen some of the stuff on Pete, for he said, "We'd look good in Technicolor."

"Maybe this is just a movie," Pete said. "Maybe you're Van Johnson and everything's going to be all right."

Williams shrugged. "What happens now, Pete?"

"We get sunk."

They watched the bridge. When the signal

came down, Pete and Williams moved with the smoothness of machinery and five torpedoes slid out of the tubes, splashed down into the water. Pete watched them, waiting to see if they were going in hot and straight.

He never found out. Something—a chimney falling, an earthquake, a stroke of lightning—threw him violently away from where he had been, smashed him against a barbette, and rolled him into the scuppers. From there, as acrid smoke cleared away, he saw that the bridge of the *Hoel* had been blasted off. It was just gone, with nothing but sky above the tangled steel which had held it up.

Pete got to his feet slowly. "Wild Bill" Williams climbed over some buckled deck plates. "She's sinking," he said.

But before she did, the *Hoel* swung slowly around and fired at the enemy with all the guns she had which would still fire. Then she fired again.

She hit them and they hit her again. Pete felt the hot, harsh sucking of the air as the shells plunged into the depths of the *Hoel*. When the yellow explosion cleared, the *Hoel* wasn't there.

The destroyer escort *Roberts* got it next. She shuddered when the shells smacked her, but staggered on for a few seconds before she simply came apart with a blast which flattened the sea around her.

Then the *Johnston* went down and only the *Heerman* fired her fish and got away alive.

Four little ships and one got away. The men who died in them gave the carriers a few seconds out of eternity and they used them well to blast the Japanese fleet with their airplanes.

The battle off Samar moved on across the swirling water and left behind the debris of war. Bits of ships, pieces of ruined planes, oil, a crate of potatoes, and men, both living and dead, floated in the long, slow-moving waves.

It was late in the afternoon when Pete Martin began again to think clearly. Far away the sun was setting, moving slowly down toward the blue haze of the Philippine Islands. As the waves passed under him, they lifted him skyward with the speed and smoothness of a plane and he could look out over the empty, littered sea before they dropped him down again into a world of darkening water.

Pete thought that his left arm had been torn off, but he couldn't be sure because he was holding Williams's head out of the water with his right arm. All the colored dye had long ago been washed off Williams's face and it was pale gray and without life. But under Pete's fingers he could still feel the irregular heartbeat.

Pete was tired and sick and holding Williams was an ordeal which he knew he could not endure much longer. And, when the sun was almost

gone, Pete wondered why he kept on holding
Williams up, wondered why he didn't let him
go—and go himself. The sea was empty and the
night was coming. Pete knew that he could not
live through the long night, and that they could
not find him in the darkness.

And then, from nowhere, a lifeboat reeled
down the back of a wave and a man with a grin
said, "Boy, we almost passed you up. Why didn't
you wave?"

"With what?" Pete asked. "This arm's busy
and that one's gone."

But Pete's arm wasn't entirely gone and the
medics in Pearl Harbor fixed it up for him almost as good as new. And they got Williams back
on his feet. . . .

And here I am, Pete thought, commanding
officer of a ship, with Wild Bill Williams down
in the engine room of her.

Pete worked his way over to the voice tubes
and flipped open the one marked ENGINE ROOM.
Cupping his hand over it to keep the water out,
he yelled, "Mr. Williams, please."

"Williams, aye, aye."

"How you makin' down there, Bill?"

"Picnic," Williams said. "Warm and dry."

"Want to go home?"

"Naw. My boys are learning a lot."

"Did you know it was wet and miserable up
here?" Pete asked.

10

"What happens to you swabbies is no concern of mine."

Pete laughed and shut the tube. When he straightened up, he found Randle at his elbow.

"Going home, Captain?" Randle asked.

Pete was about to answer when a hollow, flat, unhuman sound came out of another voice tube. "Lookout to bridge. Capsized boat two points off the port bow, sir."

Pete leaned to the tube and said, "Good work," then he peered out against the wind and sea. He could just make out a floating mass a little grayer than the water.

"Let's take a look at that," he said to Randle.

"Nothing but junk," Randle said. "This water around Cuba is always full of it."

"Might be somebody around it," Pete said.

The exec laughed. "In this weather, Captain? A mermaid couldn't live out there."

Pete glanced at his executive officer, then went across the bridge to the helmsman. "Work her up to windward of that stuff floating to port," he ordered. Then he called the engine room. "Stand by for quick changes in speed, please."

Randle came across the bridge and stood beside him as the PC wallowed down the back of a wave. "Looks like one of those Cuban fishing sloops," Randle said. "They're always going adrift in bad weather. Nice way to stave in your bow."

Pete said nothing as he studied the gray mass.

He could now make out the almost keelless hull of a deep-bellied boat and soon he could see the gray sail wallowing in the water.

"Don't see anything," Randle said. "Shall I put her back on course, Captain?"

"Circle it, please," Pete said.

The exec glared but Pete ignored him as the PC, rolling wildly in the cross sea, circled the capsized sailboat.

A body, half submerged, was lashed in the lee of the counter. The dark skin was wet and shiny, gray hair was plastered on the head. Near it was another body also lashed to the hulk.

"Both dead," Randle said.

"Get the starboard boat over, please," Pete said, trying not to let any of his irritation get into his voice. Then he asked the engine room to pump a little oil for a slick when he gave the word.

The men in the careening boat had a very hard time getting the two bodies aboard, but at last they did and worked their way back to the ship.

Pete turned the bridge over to the executive officer and went below to the tiny, hard-white sick bay. On one bunk there was the dead body of a Cuban of about twenty-five. His skull had been broken. On the other bunk a man, much older, lay with his arms across his chest. He was unconscious but alive.

Pete stooped and looked at the old man's face

and then held his wrist, feeling the faint pulsing of his blood.

The pharmacist's mate said, "I can't find anything wrong with him, Captain. Just shock from exposure and exhaustion. He's pretty old."

"Do what you can for him," Pete said. Then he noticed that around the man's waist was a light chain and to this was attached a flat, rectangular box which was completely covered with what looked like hardened tar.

"Must be his money," the pharmacist's mate said.

"Probably," Pete said. "I'll take it up to the safe." He unbuckled the chain from around the man's waist and went out carrying the box.

On the way back to the bridge Pete put the box and chain in his cabin. On the bridge he told the exec to return to Key West and then took up his station against the gun shield.

It was much easier going home before the wind. The movements of the ship were more violent, but she was not being beaten by the waves.

Pete sent a messenger to Communications with a message for an ambulance to meet them at the dock and another message telling Naval Intelligence that he was bringing an injured alien into the United States.

The messenger came back with word from sick bay that the old man was raving about his box. Pete climbed down the ladder and went below.

At the door to sick bay the pharmacist's mate said, "Captain, the old fellow thinks we stole his box."

"All right," Pete said. "It's up in my cabin. Get it and bring it down here, will you?"

The old man was trying to sit up and when he saw Pete he began croaking in Spanish. Pete, who had learned Spanish when he worked a summer on a Cuban sugar plantation, explained that the box was safe and the old man subsided. When the pharmacist's mate came in, the old man grabbed the box and hugged it with both arms.

Then he began to cry as he sat hugging the box and looking at the sheet which covered the dead man in the other bunk.

"That is my son. My last son," he said in Spanish. "Now I am all that remains."

"He's in pretty bad shape, Captain," the pharmacist's mate said. "He ought to lie down and take it easy."

Pete told the old man to lie down and the pharmacist's mate gave him a sedative. Pete put the chain back around him and left him with his box.

On his way topside Pete met Williams in the wardroom.

"Can't take it, eh?" Wild Bill said. "Running for shelter like a fair-weather sailor."

Pete shook his head. "Picked up two Cubans.

One dead, and an old one who doesn't look too healthy."

"Oh. So that was the reason for all the maneuvering around."

"Yeah. The old man was about to go wild when I took away a box he had. Thing all covered with tar to keep out the water, I suppose. And not very heavy. Must be his life's savings."

"Probably," Bill said. "Well, I'll confess. I'm about ready to go home. Half the watch below is seasick; we busted an oil line and messed the joint up for fair, and you deck hands hit every wave in the ocean."

"Warm and dry, you said," Pete reminded him.

"You ought to come down there in heavy weather, Pete. Man, it's worse than the crazy house at Coney Island. I hope on my next ship they put me on deck."

"Probably will. High time you found out who really works aboard a ship."

"Yes, sir, Captain. Aye, aye, sir, Captain. Will there be anything else, sir, Captain?"

Pete laughed and went on up to the bridge.

2

Beware The Tall One

At 0230 in the morning the pharmacist's mate woke Pete up. "Captain, the old man isn't doing very well," he said.

"I'll be right down."

Pete noticed on his way below that the weather had eased. The ship was riding with less violence and the wind was a low, deep moan in her rigging. Pete hated the night on ships at war because the blackout made the air inside them incredibly hot and foul.

In the little sick bay the air felt as though you could slice it and stack it up in slabs.

The old man was lying on his bunk, the box still hugged to his chest. When Pete leaned over him, he opened his eyes slowly and whispered, *"Capitán. Capitán."*

"Señor," Pete said.

"My life is going away," the old man said in Spanish. "He has, at last, killed us all. My wife, my beloved sons—and now he has killed me also."

"Delirious," Pete said to the pharmacist's mate. "Is there anything you can do for him?"

"I've done everything the book says, Captain."

The old man's voice had a tinge of anger in it. "Listen! Listen!" he ordered. "We were escaping from him, but the storm was too great for our little ship. Now everything is ended."

The old man closed his eyes for a moment and when he opened them and went on talking his voice was so low Pete could hardly hear the soft Spanish words.

"He has won. He has killed us all. But he still has not taken from us the book. . . . It is here." The old man's fingers tightened on the tar-covered box.

"Who?" Pete asked.

The old man did not seem to hear him. "Listen," he said. "It lies in the ocean. Near the two islands. He doesn't know where it is. No one knows except the book." Suddenly the old man raised his hand and clutched Pete's arm. "He must not get it! You must keep it away from him."

"I don't understand," Pete said. "Take your time, sleep. You can tell me in the morning."

"There is no time!" the old man said. "You must listen. This is the book of my ancestor. It is the book of the *Santa Ybel*. Because he wants it, he has burned my house, he has murdered my sons."

"Who?" Pete asked. "Who?"

But the old man's voice went slowly on. "When we had saved enough money, my sons and I, to buy a ship we went to Havana. But he was there. He asked us many questions. 'Why do you want such a ship? For what do you want apparatus to go beneath the sea?' Somehow he found out that we had this book. He took away our money and gave us no ship. He followed us. Wherever we went—into the mountains, on the seashore, in the jungles—he came also, killing us one by one to get this book."

"What's his name?" Pete asked. "Who is he?"

"The tall one," the old man said. "Beware him. To get this book he will do anything. Now . . . take it, for I can never go to the two islands."

"What's he talking about?" the pharmacist's mate asked.

"Search me," Pete said.

18

They stood and watched as the old man's eyes slowly closed. His hands relaxed and slid down the edges of the flat box.

"Take care of him," Pete said.

The pharmacist's mate shrugged.

It was just before dawn when Pete was waked up again.

"He never came to," the pharmacist's mate said. "I did everything I knew, sir."

"He was old and had been in the water a long time," Pete said. "Nobody could have saved him, Phillips."

"I hope you're right, Captain. But . . . if we'd had a doctor . . ."

Pete shook his head. "I've seen a lot of people die of shock who had had less exposure than that. And were much younger. Go turn in now."

"Aye, aye, sir." The pharmacist's mate put the box and chain down on Pete's open desk and went out.

For a while Pete lay in the darkness trying to go back to sleep. But after twelve hours of being shut up light-tight the ship's air was as foul as the inside of a cheese and Pete couldn't sleep. In nothing but skivvy pants he got up, turned on the light, and examined the box. With sweat pouring down his chest and back, he cut a slit in the pliant tar and pried off the wooden top of the box. Inside it there was a thin book bound in cowhide which had places where the hair had been eaten or worn off.

Pete took the book out and opened it under the desk light.

The ink of the writing had faded to a thin, pale brown and the penmanship was very fancy, with loops and curlicues all over the place. Slowly Pete made out the words in old Spanish:

THE LOG
of
HIS SPANISH MAJESTY'S SHIP
SANTA YBEL
On her voyage to New Spain
In the year 1519
Roberto Narvez, Navigator

Pete turned a few of the pages, which were covered with the thin, spidery writing. He stopped at one and read, slowly translating the ancient Spanish:

. . . Admiral Frederico Halivera y Martinez came aboard this date from Habana to command the ship. As soon as stores are loaded we sail for the kingdom of Montezuma far to the west. It is said that in that place gold lies about on the shores of the sea for any man to pick up and carry away. . . .

Pete turned a few more pages and stopped again to read.

. . . The loading of the treasures taken away from the rebellious Captain Cortez is now finished. Never before have such things been seen in the world and, for fear that I may be doubted, I list here only those things which I have seen with my own eyes:

A very curious and cleverly contrived statue which is a snake with the wings of a bird. The eyes of the snake are precious stones and the whole statue is of solid gold much chased and engraved.

A wheel, or disk, of solid gold which is very thick through, measuring more than a half arm's length and of a diameter greater than two arms' length. The whole surface curiously inscribed with many figures of men, animals, and strange symbols. The Mexican prisoners, which we have also captured and taken on board, declare that this curious thing is used by the Aztec people to predict the future of the world.

A great multitude of birds and animals made entirely of gold and precious stones and so cleverly designed that they much resemble living things and are of the same size. These are most beautifully made.

Many utensils for eating, of such workmanship as even His Majesty has never seen. There are plates, platters, and goblets as well as knives and ladles made all of gold and wonderfully chased and designed.

Ornaments worn by these Aztec people made of gold and precious stones . . .

Pete wiped the sweat off his face with a towel and turned the pages.

. . . On this day one of the Mexican prisoners disappeared from the ship. A search has been made of every part, but he has not been discovered. Therefore, in his grief at being made a prisoner, he must have leaped into the sea. Now that he has gone the other prisoners have disclosed that he was the nephew of Montezuma, who was the king of the Aztecs, and that his name was Uemac. It is indeed sorrowful that a person of such distinction should have taken his life in this manner, for upon our arrival in Spain he would have had much made of him and even perhaps have been presented to His Majesty. But these are a strange and violent people.

In his mind's eye Pete could imagine the great Spanish galleon going full and by across the Gulf of Mexico. In the ornate cabins, hung like bird cages under the stern overhang, Admiral Halivera would be rubbing his hands at the thought of the treasures he had stolen. Roberto Narvez, in the dingy midships, would be writing in his journal or working out the crude dead-reckoning position of his ship. The Mexican prisoners—"strange and violent"—would be below somewhere in a noisome hold. Pete couldn't share Narvez's opinion about Uemac. He had probably been a wild, proud man, the nephew of a great king, whose soul could not endure slavery under the Spaniards.

Pete turned a few more pages.

. . . Water is reported coming into the ship by the sailing master. The admiral is very angry and paces about the deck while even the navigator has been ordered below to search for the leak. Every part of the ship is being searched except the compartment in which the treasure is stored. This place, being sealed by the admiral himself, cannot be opened.

Pete turned to the next day.

. . . The sailing master was, alas, correct. His insistence, even in the face of the admiral's anger, that the leak was in the hold where the treasure is stored, has been proven correct. With the admiral's permission and with a body of Marines to insure that none of the treasure would be stolen, that compartment was opened and found to be flooded with water.

A strange thing was also found to be there. Uemac, the prisoner who disappeared, was there. The water, filling slowly the whole of the compartment, had, at last, drowned him. The carpenter declares that Uemac is somehow responsible for the water coming into the ship, for he declares that the bottom is very sound and only a man opening it could allow the water to enter. I cannot agree with the carpenter, for how could a man with no implement other than, perhaps, a knife cut through the stout timbers of the ship's bottom strakes?

We will determine if the carpenter is correct in his accusation of the dead man when we have pumped out all the water now in that compartment.

Pete was startled by the boatswain's pipe and the voice on the loudspeaker saying, "Relieve the watch." For a little while, reading the old book, he had almost been living back there on the galleon, taking part in the strange things which had happened there.

Pete read more rapidly, skipping over the words he could not easily make out.

. . . The ship is sinking very swiftly now. The efforts of all the men and even the prisoners upon the pumps have been to no avail, for the water has risen steadily in the ship during the entire night and this much of the day.

This is all that I can write in this log, for I am preparing now to leave this ill-fated ship. I will be able to take with me only a little water and a little bread and I will wrap this log in my best silk scarf and soak it in paraffin, hoping thus to preserve it against the moisture of the sea.

I have most carefully determined the position of the ship. Although I cannot see them, there are upon the chart two islands to the eastward, one of them distant four leagues, the other nearly five. These islands I remember seeing on the outward voyage and one is barren and small, whereas the other is larger and with vegetation upon it.

May God grant me strength to survive the perils of the sea.

Pete slowly closed the book on this last page and sat for a moment staring blankly at the steel bulkhead of his cabin. In his hands he held the log, so Narvez, the young navigator, must have survived the perils of the sea and, sometime, he must have been rescued from one of the islands.

Or perhaps, Pete thought, the *Santa Ybel* had not gone down after all. Perhaps with all hands and the Mexican prisoners on the pumps they had managed to keep her afloat until they reached shore.

But, he argued, what about the old man down there in sick bay? Somehow, century after century, the book had stayed in the Narvez family and, generation after generation, they had be-

24

lieved that the *Santa Ybel* went down with the Aztec treasure. Perhaps the young navigator had somehow reached Cuba and had stayed there, got married, had children. And each generation had been brought up with the legend of the *Santa Ybel* a living part of their lives.

Or, Pete decided, the whole thing was a hoax. But when he remembered the old man whispering in the middle of the night, he could not believe it.

Then what was all this about the "tall one"?

Pete sat trying to remember exactly what the old man had said. What was that about saving up money to get a ship? And what had he said about "apparatus to go beneath the sea"?

Slowly, remembering the book, remembering the old man's whispering, Pete pieced together a picture. Somewhere in Cuba old Narvez and his sons had worked for years and saved every peso. Ahead of them always was the *Santa Ybel* lying on the bottom of the sea, and to reach her they knew that they must have a fairly large ship and one equipped with gear for locating the wreck and more gear for diving down to her.

So at last they had saved up enough money. "We went to Havana," the old man had said. He and his sons. They had inquired about buying a ship. Pete could easily understand how a shipbroker would get very curious when an old Cuban peasant began pricing ships for diving.

So, Pete decided, that's where the "tall one" came in. Some unscrupulous man had figured out that Narvez knew where treasure was. Probably figured that Narvez had an old chart or just such a book as this log. And had tried to get it. He had not stopped at arson or murder and, at last, he had driven Narvez and his last son into the storm which had cost them their lives.

Nice guy, Pete thought.

Then Pete stood up, closed his desk on the book, and began to dress. "Let's get on with the war, Martin," he said, half aloud.

The storm had ended and the Gulf was calm as a sleeping baby. Pete took a quick breather and then went into the wardroom for breakfast. Williams was already there, eating late like most Black Gang officers; the other officers had finished and gone on deck.

"I've got something I'd like to show you, Bill," Pete said. "That is—if you've got time after you finish scoffing chow."

"The captain's wish is my command, sir," Williams said.

Pete glowered at him. "I hope someday that the Navy Department will make a mistake and let you be commanding officer of a ship, son. Only then will you understand what a burden you junior officers can be."

"Don't 'junior officer' me, lad," Williams said.

26

"These things may be tarnished by honest sweat, but they're still the railroad tracks which designate a lieutenant of the most senior grade." Then he rubbed his collar insignia with his napkin and stood up when Pete did.

"In my desk is an old book, Bill. How about taking a look at it while I see that my precious ship is all in one piece and none of the ensigns are crying with homesickness?"

"Okay, Grandma," Williams said.

Pete went on the bridge to take the eight o'clock reports, then he checked the departments and saw that the liberty section had been posted. In the Communications Office he countermanded his request for an ambulance, reported the death at sea, and notified Naval Intelligence. It took him nearly an hour to check everything and, when he got back to his cabin, Williams was still sitting at his desk, his head propped on his palms and reading so deeply that he didn't even hear Pete come in.

"What do you think of it, Bill?" Pete asked.

Williams slowly closed the book and swung around in the chair. "Where'd it come from?"

"The old Cuban had it. He died last night." Pete nodded toward the empty box.

"Too bad."

Pete told him about the midnight talk with old Narvez; about the "tall one" and the sons.

Williams slowly shook his head. "I don't

know," he said. "Might be a put-up job. I don't see why, though, because nobody gets anything and when these things are faked it's generally for a purpose—sucker bait. My Spanish isn't as good as yours so I can't tell whether it's really old Castilian or not. Can you?"

Pete shook his head. "All the Spanish I know is what I learned in Cuba."

"Of course, the old man might have been just a stooge for somebody. He might have been on his way to plant this thing when the storm hit them."

"Maybe, but I don't think so, Bill. For a man to put to sea in that boat in that storm, he would have to have something really driving him, something on shore which was a lot worse than the danger of the storm."

"Guess you're right. Listen, Pete, my father knows more about this stuff than anybody in the world. You know he used to be in the ship-salvage business before he got all broken up in Valparaiso. Since then he's spent most of his time studying old logs, histories, fairy tales about sunken ships. If this thing is genuine, he'll know it because he knows the name of every ship that ever sailed from Spain; he knows where they went and, if they didn't come back, what is supposed to have happened to them. If there ever was a *Santa Ybel* in the Spanish navy, my dad will know about it.

"So how about letting me take this thing and show it to him, Pete? I promise you that no one else will see it, or even know it exists. But I warn you, if Dad thinks it's genuine, he'll want to get up an expedition to go find it the minute the war's over."

"I wish you would, Bill. I'm just curious about it, that's all." Pete laughed. "After all, I've got the war to win, you know."

"That so? I thought you'd already won it." Then Williams grinned. "The obvious thing to do, Captain, is to give poor old Wild Bill Williams a little leave, Captain, sir. Then he can go over to Miami and consult with his father."

"Okay, you dog. Make out some leave papers."

Williams was wrapping up the book when the communications officer, a young ensign who took himself very seriously, knocked on the door. He came in with a radioman third class who looked as though he had just seen a rattlesnake in his bed.

"Captain," the ensign said, "I request permission to put this man, Roark, on report for improper performance of duty."

"That's pretty serious, Mr. Jenkins," Pete said. "Tell me about it."

"Well, sir, yesterday when we were maneuvering around that wrecked sailboat Roark here was on watch in the sound room. He picked up a ship of some kind within four miles of us and that sailboat and—sir, he did not report it to anyone. He did enter it in the log."

Pete looked at Roark, who was getting paler and paler. "At ease, Roark," he said. "How long have you been standing top watches in the sound room, Roark?"

"That . . . that was my first one, sir."

"Did you know that you were supposed to report any sound to the bridge?"

"Yes, sir."

"But you didn't report this one?"

"No, sir. You see, sir, I was watching them trying to get those people into the lifeboat, sir, and I just forgot about the other ship."

"What did it sound like, Roark?"

"Oh, it wasn't a submarine, sir. It was a single-engined craft, engine idling, and it sounded very small and—not very dangerous, sir."

"Well, that's all, Roark. Just watch it in the future, will you?" Pete said.

"Oh yes, sir. I certainly will."

Roark almost ran out of the cabin. Pete said to Ensign Jenkins, "How about letting him off this time? He's new and young."

"If you wish, Captain. But I will certainly keep an eye on him."

"Do that," Pete said.

When he had gone out, Pete looked at Williams.

"The tall one?" Williams said.

"Could be," Pete said. "It isn't too fantastic to think that the 'tall one' followed Narvez and was about to close in on him when we came along. I can't explain a small single-engined boat out in such weather any other way."

"More likely a Coast Guard job," Williams said. "But if it *was* Narvez's little playmate, he now knows where the log is. And it wouldn't take much genius to figure out that the commanding officer of a ship would take charge of personal effects. In other words, Pete boy, you're 'it' from now on out."

Pete took the log and slipped it into a big brown manila envelope. He glued the flap down and handed it to Williams. "Your baby, Bill. And if I'm going to play a game of tag such as that joker played with Narvez, I'd feel a lot better if I knew who he was and what he looks like."

"So would I. But I don't think he plays that way. He sounds like one of these ice-knife-in-the-back boys."

Pete suddenly laughed. "We sound like people in a B movie. The whole thing is a hoax. Take it along to your papa and let him make it official."

3

Top Secret

As soon as Pete's PC moored in Key West and the gangplank went down, a very official-looking Marine came aboard with a message for the commanding officer. Pete was in his cabin taking a shower, and the Marine waited.

When Pete came out of the shower with a bath towel around his hips, the Marine was lounging in the doorway. He went stiff as a pole at the sight of Pete, saluted, and said, "The admiral would like to see you immediately, sir."

"Very well," Pete said. "Stand by on the dock, please."

"Aye, aye, sir." The Marine smacked his heels together sharply and went out.

Before the cabin curtains stopped swinging, the exec knocked and came in. "What's up, Captain?" he asked.

"Admiral wants to see me—immediately," Pete said.

The exec whistled through his teeth. "Want me to come along and pick up the pieces?" he asked.

Pete shook his head. "Stay aboard, please."

As Pete rigged his uniform, putting on the brand-new two-and-a-half stripe shoulder boards and then pinning his ribbons above the left breast pocket, the exec hung around. "Think you're in trouble, Captain?" he asked.

"Possibly. I generally am," Pete said, pinning the Purple Heart and the Navy Cross above the pre-Pearl Harbor, American and Pacific Theater ribbons, and the Philippine Liberation with star. Then he was ready to go. Shining the toes of his shoes on the calves of his legs, he started out.

"I hope the admiral doesn't take your command away from you," the exec said. "But that business yesterday was pretty foolish."

Pete turned in the doorway and faced his exec. Then he decided that this was not the time to start straightening out the exec, and he went on down the passageway.

The admiral was walking up and down in the small office when Pete opened the door and went in. Two fans set on the floor made a humming noise but didn't do much about the heat.

Pete stood at attention, his cap in his hand, and said, "Good morning, Admiral."

"Carry on," the admiral said, sitting down at his desk. "How's that ship of yours?"

"Fine, sir."

"How do you like this milk-run duty?"

Pete smiled a little. "It's a vacation, sir."

The admiral laughed. "Want to get back in the fightin' war, Martin?"

Pete studied the admiral's thin, intelligent face and wondered what was coming next. "I'd like to go back to the Pacific as a—commanding officer, Admiral," Pete said.

"All right," the admiral said. Then he got up and began to walk up and down again. "Do one more job down here, and we'll send you out."

"Aye, aye, sir."

"Tonight some civilians are coming aboard your ship to install an underwater detector, Martin. The thing is absolutely top secret; so I want you to set up space for it and keep an armed guard on it around the clock. I want no one to even look at that thing except you and the special operator we're sending along with it."

"Aye, aye, sir."

"In case you get into any kind of trouble,

destroy it. There are electric detonators rigged into it, and the operator has instructions to obey you."

The admiral sat down again. "The Bureau of Ships claims that this detector is absolutely cold forty. They claim that it can locate a ten-cent piece in a hundred fathoms on a dark night. We've got submarines to operate with you on the test runs and we also want you to see if it will locate subs that we think we've sunk around in the Gulf. Here's a chart with the sunk subs spotted in on it." He handed Pete a rolled-up chart.

"As soon as you give this thing a real workout, I'll get you back into the shootin' war, and I'll get you out of the PCs and into subchasers. Or would you rather ride as exec on a destroyer escort or even one of the small cans?"

"I'd rather be commanding officer if it's only a raft," Pete said.

"I would too," the admiral said. "C.O.'s the best job in the Navy. . . . All right, the civilians will be down there now. And remember, Martin, this is top secret."

"I will, Admiral."

As Pete turned to leave the admiral asked, "How old are you, Martin?"

"Twenty-four, sir."

"You must be the youngest two-and-a-half-striper in the Navy."

Pete shook his head. "There must be a lot of the zoomie boys younger than I am, Admiral."

The admiral leaned back and laughed. "They don't count," he said.

Back aboard his ship Pete watched as the civilian workers installed the supersonic detector. He had had a small compartment emptied for the thing, and the metalsmith was welding a new hasp so that it could be locked. Pete got all the keys for the new lock from the first lieutenant and had the exec arrange with the division officers to keep a heel-and-toe watch on the door.

Going back to his cabin, he unrolled the chart and studied the positions of the submarines marked in red ink. These were the German subs which had presumably been sunk, and Pete planned the next day's cruise to take in as many of the positions as he could.

When he finished, he sat back in the soft chair, put his feet up on the desk panel, and stared at the gray steel overhead. The pit of his stomach began to feel cold as he thought about going back into the Pacific. He began to remember that October day aboard the *Hoel;* he heard the swhoosh of the salvo coming in. Pete thought, If I'd just said to the admiral, "I've had enough shootin', Admiral. I've done my share. . . ." Pete thought about Randle, the exec. For almost three years Randle had been riding ships in water as safe as his grandmama's bathtub. Why couldn't they get the feather merchants into the war?

Then all that went away and Pete realized that, actually, he would be glad to go out again. The monotony of the milk-run was getting him down. The sloppiness of the feather merchants, the red tape, and all the rest of it were worse than the terrible nights and days in enemy water.

Pete lowered his feet and stood up. Out loud he said, "Ole Pete Martin's goin' back to dee wah." He looked at his serious face in the mirror and suddenly laughed. Then he got serious again as he saw the dull purple on the ribbon. "But I don't want a star on that Purple Heart," he said quietly.

He put the chart in the safe, turned the dial, and went below to watch them rig the detector.

The heavy weather of the day before was gone and the Gulf of Mexico, as though apologizing for its bad behavior, was as calm as a millpond. As soon as Pete conned his ship into open water, he turned the bridge over to the officer of the deck and went down to the little compartment.

It was stinking hot in there, and the operator was sweating through his dungarees. Pete sent the messenger for an electrician's mate, who came soon and installed a fan.

"Is this thing as good as they claim it is?" Pete asked the operator.

"It was good on shore, sir. The test runs in the lab were really something!"

"How does it work?"

"There's nothing new about it, sir. It's just a h o p p e d - u p sounding device. Instead of using sound waves going down to the bottom and be-  ing caught in a receiver on the way back, this one uses electronics. Nothing interferes with them on the way down and back, and it is much faster. As you go along, you get a very accurate picture of the whole area on this screen."

Pete watched the wavering lines of pale green on the dark, curved screen. "Can you measure length and depth with it? I mean, if you get a hump—say a sub—can you measure how long it is and how thick?"

"Yes, sir. This scale gives you the distance of whatever you're looking at from the bottom of the ship. That gives you a constant to use in interpolating the dimensions of the object." The operator turned and grinned at Pete. "Anyway, that's what they told me."

"Well, we'll give it a workout," Pete said.

One by one they found the submarines which had been marked on the chart as "Sure." Pete spent the day between the bridge and the detector room and by the time they knocked off for the night he was convinced that the detector was good. In each area marked "Sure" the wavery green lines had perfectly outlined the hull of a submarine. They were unmistakable—long, thin, and, if on their sides, even the conning tower was outlined.

Before turning in Pete wrote up the Night Book and then prepared his courses for the next day's work, which would be to the west of Cuba where the Nazi subs had made their wolf-pack runs on the Gulf coast shipping. There were not many "Sure" kills in the area because most of the subs had been attacked by aircraft from the land and they could not verify a kill the way destroyers and subchasers could with sonic apparatus.

By noon the next day they had found subs at two "Sures" and two "Probables" but, after careful searching, had found nothing in areas of one "Probable" and two "Doubtfuls."

"Chow down," Pete said to the operator. "After chow we'll work out these three and I think that'll satisfy all hands, don't you?"

"Yes, sir."

"Tomorrow we'll get the base to send out some subs and we'll work on them. I wouldn't be surprised if this gadget gives 'em a bad time."

The operator grinned. "They won't have a chance. We'll be all over them like a blanket."

Feeling a little sleepy from eating too much, Pete sat with his feet propped on a wastebasket while the exec conned the ship back and forth through a square of water. In June 1943 a torpedo-plane, fighter-plane team had reported a probable kill but had not given a very good fix on it.

"Don't believe the airedales got that one," the operator said.

Pete watched the screen. "Doesn't look like it."

"Did you notice the drop she took, sir? The bottom is almost flat at a hundred and ten feet and then it breaks off as sharp as a knife blade and goes down to nearly a thousand."

"Must have missed that," Pete said. "Watching that thing makes me sleepy. Let's run over it again." He phoned the bridge and then watched the thin lines as the ship changed course.

"Now watch," the operator said.

Suddenly, with no warning, the ocean floor reflected in the screen went from a hundred to a thousand feet.

"Let's run along the edge of that," Pete said, phoning a change of course to the bridge.

Pete watched the screen as the ship moved inch by inch, the screws barely turning over.

Suddenly the lines humped up a little, ran roughly for about two hundred feet, then sloped down to level bottom again.

"Wonder what that was?" the operator said. "Can we go back over that, sir?"

Pete ordered a 180 turn.

As the green line humped up again the operator made swift notes. As the line leveled off he said, "Something down there about two hundred and fifty-five feet long and forty feet thick. Funny shape for a sub, isn't it, sir?"

"Pretty tubby," Pete said.

"Can we take a run across it, sir?"

Pete gave the order and the ship turned.

"Wow!" the operator said. "Look at that. Whatever ship that is, she went down right on the brink of that deep. It looks like two more feet to the south and she would have gone down another thousand feet."

They ran back over it again and this time, after the line dipped down into the chasm, it picked up something else. Pete had the ship sail a grid over it and the operator said at last, "That's a sub, all right. The airedales got it after all."

Pete got up and went over to the admiral's chart. Underneath the "Probable" he wrote carefully the latitude and longitude of the submarine and the depth—1020 feet. As he finished he looked at the chart for the next search.

His writing, the numbers of the latitude and longitude, ran through the shaded area which marked an island. Near that was another shaded area. Two islands. Two small islands.

Suddenly, as though Narvez's log was in front of him, Pete saw the spidery Spanish writing. ". . . there are upon the chart two islands to the eastward, one of them distant four leagues, the other nearly five. . . ."

Pete didn't know how long he had been standing there staring at the chart, wondering if that shape, that mass of something lying on the brink of the sea's chasm, was the hulk of the *Santa Ybel*. A league was about three miles and the distances were approximately right. Two islands . . . two small islands . . . lying to the eastward. "One is barren," the log had said, "and small, whereas the other is larger and with vegetation upon it. . . ."

"What next, sir?" the operator asked.

It brought Pete back into the hot little room. "Er—let's call it a day. Shut her down and let's get some air."

As Pete climbed up to the open bridge, he found that his knees were shaking a little. On the bridge the exec moved to his side as Pete went to the shield.

Pete was almost afraid to look through the big telescope mounted on its stand, but at last he put his eye against the rubber piece and slowly swung the scope eastward.

"Put her on 90. Standard," Pete ordered.

The engines began to throb, white water sliced away at the bows. Pete watched the horizon with the glass and slowly, almost like small, low clouds, the islands appeared.

Pete was holding his breath and his knees were shaking again.

One island was very small and not so much as a blade of grass grew on it. The other island was dark green with palm trees bending above it and a little lagoon formed by an arm of coral.

For a long time Pete studied the two islands as the ship passed between them. Then he put the caps back on the scope and rigged it inboard.

Then he went down to the detector room again, let himself in, and locked the door. Standing in front of the chart, he memorized the numbers he had written on it so that he would never forget them.

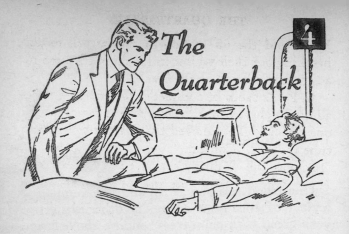

The Quarterback

Pete tested the device for seven more days. As he and the operator got more familiar with it and learned to interpret the wavery green lines, Pete began to believe in the infallibility of the gadget. Working with stuff on the bottom, it was almost miraculous and, during the last few days, when they worked with moving submarines, it caught them every time.

"Wish we'd had this thing when Hitler was ending his wolf packs in here," Pete said. "And he Japoons had better stand back when we put his doohickey in the Pacific."

"I used to think I'd like to serve in subs," the perator said. "But after watching this thing . . ."

"Shut her down," Pete said. On the phone to ie bridge he said, "Take her home."

The PC turned her sharp bows toward Key

44

West, and the off section of the watch began breaking out their whites and looking forward to a few days' liberty on the beach.

In Pete's cabin he completed the entries on the admiral's chart and, as he was rolling it up, someone knocked. Pete shoved the chart into its steel tube and said, "Come in."

It was Bill Williams's assistant, a lieutenant (j.g.), younger than Pete and a genius with engines. Pete liked him. He was a quiet, studious man who never said very much. And he was a first-class officer. He had served in cans in the Pacific and knew the score.

"Afternoon, Captain," Walsh said.

"Sit down, Sandy," Pete said, waving at the bunk. "What's the trouble?"

Walsh smiled shyly. "Shivering shaft, Captain. Don't know if Mr. Williams mentioned it, but I think we're going to have to lay her up for a while."

"All right. I'll see if we can get availability." Pete called in the messenger and sent a dispatch requesting space in the repair yard up to Communications. "It'll give the crew a little breather on the beach. They've been at sea pretty steadily during the last month."

Pete glanced at the calendar on his desk and saw that he hadn't changed the months. He ripped off July and dropped it in the wastebasket.

"August 3, 1945," he said. "I've been in the Navy exactly four years and twenty minutes."

"You've got a year on me," Walsh said. "What's this scuttlebutt about you going back to the Pacific, Captain?"

"Soon," Pete said.

"Want to?"

Pete grinned. "Scared to death."

"I am too," Walsh said. "But I'm fed to the eyes on this training racket. 'This is a valve, gentlemen. This is a piston. It goes up and down.'"

Pete laughed. "The way they were throwing kamikazes at Okinawa last month, they won't have any left by the time I get out there. I'm scared of those buzzards."

Walsh lit a cigarette and blew a smoke ring. "Don't you think it's winding up, Captain?"

Pete nodded. "But if that stubborn streak holds out, it'll be a long time. The little yellow monkeys don't know when they're whipped." Pete grinned at Walsh. "I think there'll be plenty of time for you and me both to sweat out another tour."

"What're you going to do when it's over, Captain?"

"Search me," Pete said.

"What does your father do?"

"He's dead. He was a pilot on the early airlines. Hit a mountain in Pennsylvania."

"Sorry," Walsh said.

"How about you?"

"I'm trying to make Regular Navy. I like engines, Captain, and I like the Navy although a Reserve isn't supposed to say so."

Pete laughed. "I'll probably end up being the second assistant windshield wiper in a filling station. I've got a mother and a kid brother to support."

Walsh started to say something when the phone from the bridge rang. "Making port, Captain."

"Very well," Pete said.

"How about chow at the club tonight, Sandy?" Pete asked as he put on his cap. "Bill will be back and we'll tie one on."

"Roger, thanks."

As soon as the PC was tied up, Pete took the chart around to the admiral.

"What do you think of the gadget, Martin?" the admiral asked.

"It's a little better than they claimed it is, Admiral." He unrolled the chart and spread it out. "Where we couldn't find a sunk sub, I think there wasn't one, Admiral."

"Good work. I'd like to have a full report on it, Martin."

"In the morning, sir."

The admiral put the chart away. "I've got a ship for you," he said. "Brand spanking new and all finished with the trial and shakedown. One of the new 'chasers."

"Thanks very much, Admiral."

"Your orders are on the way."

Pete's throat felt a little dry. "Admiral, could I have a couple of days to go see my folks up in Georgia?" he asked.

"Certainly. Let's see, this is the third. Get back Tuesday night, please. That'll be the seventh."

"Aye, aye, sir. Thanks very much, Admiral."

When Pete went up the gangplank of his ship, the officer of the deck saluted him and handed him a telegram.

Pete put it in his pocket, thanked the OD, and went on to his cabin. He checked through the various reports from the division officers and was opening the telegram when Bill Williams knocked and came in.

Bill closed the door, put the log, still wrapped up, down on the desk, and said, "Dad says its genuine. HSMS *Santa Ybel* never returned to Spain and no trace of her has ever been found after she sailed from Vera Cruz, Mexico, on the twenty-second of September, 1520."

"I've got a little news, too," Pete said. "But hold up until I read this." He unfolded the telegram. It read:

JOHNNY HURT CAN YOU COME HOME.
MOTHER.

Pete gritted his teeth and read the thing again.

"Bad?" Williams asked.

"My kid brother." He handed Bill the telegram.

"What do you think happened?"

"Don't know. But Mother doesn't yell easy, Bill."

"You'd better get emergency leave."

"Just got four days from the admiral. But I've got a lot to do before I can go."

Pete rang for a messenger. "Please find Lieutenant Walsh and ask him to come up here," he told him. "And the executive officer. And the first lieutenant and the ship's clerk. Tell *him* to bring plenty of pads and pencils."

"Aye, aye, sir."

"While you were on leave, Bill, we ran some tests. The admiral wants a report tonight. And we're going in dry dock tomorrow."

"Yeah. Sandy Walsh told me. When'll you be through because I know a guy in Operations at the air station and maybe I can get you a plane ride?"

"That'd be fine. Around midnight, Bill."

"Roger. I'll be waiting for you in my car."

"Thanks a lot. Is the phone connected to shore yet?"

"Yep."

Pete explained to the Navy switchboard that

it was a personal emergency and then put in his call. As he was waiting, Sandy Walsh knocked.

"Sandy, I'm sorry as I can be, but the dinner's off. My kid brother's hurt himself and I'm going up there tonight."

"I'm sorry, Captain," Walsh said.

"Come on with me, Sandy," Williams said. "We'll give the skipper a rain check."

As Bill went out he tapped the package significantly with his finger. Pete saw him and nodded. "I'll take care of it," he said.

Then the ship's clerk came in and Pete started dictating to him the report of the experiments with the detector. "This is all top secret, Matthews," he said. "Burn your notebook and all your carbon copies when you finish."

It took more than an hour to get the call through and Pete's mind kept wandering away from the detector. He kept seeing his kid brother —a towheaded, good-looking kid who seemed to be always at the point of boiling. He did everything at top speed and with complete enthusiasm.

But at last the phone rang, and Pete picked it up. The connection was very bad, and he could hardly hear what his mother said. He thought she said something about football, but there wasn't much football played in August. He kept repeating slowly that he was coming home, and at last she understood him.

While he waited for the ship's clerk to type

up the report, he packed a few things in a suitcase. Bill Williams came back and said there was a plane standing by out at the field.

At last the report was finished. Pete sent it over to the Officer Messenger Center and then locked the log of the *Santa Ybel* in his desk safe.

In Williams's car going to the air station, Pete said, "We were testing an underwater detector, Bill, and close to two small islands it picked up a hulk of something about two hundred and fifty feet long by forty thick lying in a hundred and ten feet of water."

"What do you think?"

"I don't know how long a 'league' was in those days and the dead reckoning they used in 1519 to navigate with must have just about kept them in one ocean. But the book said the ship was sinking four leagues from one island and five from the other. Figuring a league at three nautical miles, that hulk lies just about where the *Santa Ybel* would have sunk."

"Dad says the log is the real McCoy, Pete. He looked up a lot of stuff about Cortez and the backbiting that went on between those Spaniards in Cuba and Mexico. Dad says the whole picture fits in with the known history. Cortez had been living the life of Riley in what we call Mexico City—they had some other name for it—when the Aztecs or whoever they were rose up and threw old Cortez out.

"The city was built up on an island in a big lake with dirt causeways leading to shore. When the citizens began tossing the Spaniards out, Cortez and his boys grabbed all the loot they could get. That much is in the history books. And the fact that some of Cortez's men deserted him as soon as they got on shore is in the books. What isn't in the books is what happened to the swag. Somebody made off with it and Dad thinks it was the bunch of Spaniards who deserted Cortez. Anyway, it disappeared and—so did the *Santa Ybel*."

"And," Pete said, "if that wreck near the islands is the *Santa Ybel*, all you've got to do is dive down and bring up the gold."

"Did you get a fix on it?"

"Brother, I've got the latitude and longitude down to tenths of seconds written right across my brain," Pete said.

"All right, when this unpleasantness with His Lowness, Hirohito, is over, Dad says he wants to go look for the *Santa Ybel*. Of course, he can't go—he can't even get out of a wheel chair by himself—but he's got a little money and he wants to get up an expedition to go after it."

"What about you, Bill?"

Williams twisted a big gold ring around on a finger of his left hand and shook his head. "No. I'm staying in the Navy, Pete. I'm an old Annapolis man—excuse me, Trade School boy—and

I'm making a career out of it. Always wanted to ride around in ships and the Navy is the only place you can have a ship but not pay for it."

As the car turned in to the airport, Pete said, "We're talking like a couple of civilians, Bill. Let's forget the whole thing. After all, I'm getting orders. I'm going back into the shooting war."

"You're taking me too, pal."

Pete looked at Bill's face as the beacon swung across it. "You want to go?"

"No. But who'll run your engines for you if you don't take me?"

"You'll be sorr-eee."

"Sure. But how will you get another Navy Cross if you don't have me to save again?"

Bill stopped outside the operations shack. "Give Johnny my best, Pete," he said. "And I hope it isn't serious. See you when you get back."

"Thanks. By the way, stick around while we're in dry dock and see that those hammerheads don't leave a hole in the bottom of the boat, will you?"

"I'll get 'em to put curtains over your portholes, Captain."

It was after midnight when they took off in the SNJ. Pete looked down at the moonlit, dimmed-out country sliding below, and as he got closer to Georgia, his worry about his brother grew stronger. With nothing to do in the plane, he kept imagining things which a fourteen-year-old could do to hurt himself.

At last he got home. Lights were on in the little house, and as Pete walked up the path, he saw, without noticing them, the magnolia blossoms still on the two trees.

His mother and Dr. Norfleet were standing in the living room talking when he came in. He kissed his mother and looked at her eyes. They were too dry, Pete thought.

"What happened?" he asked.

"He was playing football, Pete," his mother said. "In that field behind the ice plant. Freddy said he was running for a pass with his head turned back watching the ball, and he ran into something—a pile of junk, crates, old iron things."

Pete looked at the doctor.

"Back. Two places," the doctor said.

"Can I see him?"

"Don't stay long, Pete," the doctor said.

In his brother's quiet, hot room the moonlight made the bed look very white, and Pete wondered if the white pillow and the white sheets were what made Johnny's face look so white. All the sunburn seemed to have been drained away, and Johnny's arms, already as strong as a man's, looked limp and heavy.

Pete said quietly, "Hello, Jawn," and saw his eyes open slowly.

"Hi, Commander," Johnny said, but it was only a slow whisper.

"Hear you got fouled up."

"As a quarterback I'm a good water boy."

"Stop bragging and go to sleep, Jawn. I'll see you in the morning."

"Roger . . . wilco," Johnny whispered.

Pete shut the door softly and stood for a moment in the dark hall. A hard, painful lump was in his throat, and he swallowed twice before he went back to the living room. Pete put his arm about his mother's shoulder. "What happens now?" he asked the doctor.

"It's going to take a long, long time, Pete. Maybe he'll recover, maybe he won't. And it's going to take"—the doctor paused and looked first at Pete's mother and then up at Pete—"a whale of a lot of money. He'll have to be in a special hospital, with special doctors and nurses and expensive treatments. Lot of money, Pete."

"Okay," Pete said. "I've got a thousand now."

"That'll start it," the doctor said.

"Let's get it started then," Pete said. "What hospital has got what he needs?"

The doctor told him, and Pete said, "How about calling them up and getting space for Johnny, and I'll get an ambulance?"

When the doctor went out, Pete's mother began to cry. Not much, just softly as she sat huddled up in the chair.

The next few days were hard on Pete. To see Johnny lying there unable to move from his shoulders down, not able to talk except in a halting whisper, was bad. But the kid's courage was worse. Pete never saw a sign of fear in Johnny's eyes; he never saw the kid's lips tremble or tears come up in his eyes. Pete, after watching his brother for a few days, decided that the doctor was wrong in not telling Johnny the truth. And on the night he went into the hospital Pete told him.

Johnny lay flat on his back in the high white bed and listened, his eyes never leaving Pete's. Once Pete saw the muscles around the corners of his mouth draw tight, but he took it without a whimper.

"So that's the way it is, Jawn," Pete finished.

"Okay."

"I thought you ought to know all about it," Pete said.

"Sure. I'll work harder. I thought . . . I thought it was just sort of temporary, Pete."

"You'll get over it."

"You think so? Really, Pete?"

Pete nodded.

"That's all right then," Johnny said. "Have you got to go back to the war, Pete?"

"In the morning."

"Take care of yourself."

"Don't worry, Jawn."

"Well, take care of yourself anyway."

"I will. . . . Sack time for quarterbacks," Pete said.

Johnny grinned. "You know what I thought when I hit the trash pile, Pete? I thought, Wow, somebody has really tackled me around the shoelaces this time. But I caught the pass."

They sold the house to get money, and Pete's mother found a room in a boardinghouse in the town where the hospital was. Before dawn on August 7 Pete caught the bus for Miami. He couldn't sleep, and he watched the sun come up and the baking-hot day begin.

At the lunch stop people in the little restaurant seemed very excited about something. Pete bought an Atlanta paper and saw huge headlines: NEW BOMB WIPES OUT JAP CITY. While he waited for his lunch, he read about the destruction of Hiroshima on Honshu. One 29 had dropped one bomb—some sort of atom thing—and the entire city was demolished.

This is the end, Pete thought. We've won it. It'll wind up fast now.

Riding in the hot, lurching bus again, Pete tried to keep thinking about the future and not about Johnny lying in that narrow bed.

The war was as good as over. No nation could take the sort of pounding we could give it with the atomic bombs. One bomb—one city. The war was over, and he would be out of the Navy soon. And no more blue checks twice a month.

But at a place where a hairline of longitude crossed a hairline of latitude lay the hulk of a Spanish ship.

Pete put his head back on the rest and closed his eyes. He didn't sleep—he made his plans.

It was late at night when he found his ship. It had been hauled out on the marine railway in the repair yard, and Pete walked along the starboard side looking at the few barnacles on the plates. The whole place was lit up with floodlights and, as Pete climbed up the makeshift ladder to the quarterdeck, he could hear people inside his ship hammering and banging.

Pete went first down into the shaft alley to watch the night shift drawing the sprung shaft and replacing the big bearings. Then, tired and suddenly very sleepy, he went up to his cabin.

The curtains of the cabin hung motionless across the door, but under them there was a strip of light. Pete thought nothing of it and was about to go in when the light moved.

Pete stood for a second watching the strip of light moving. A cold shiver ran along his spine. Then, without making a sound, he drew the curtains back and stepped into his cabin.

A civilian in dirty overalls was down on his knees on the floor working at one of the deck plates with a wrench. He looked up over his shoulder as Pete came in.

"The trouble is down in the shaft alley," Pete said quietly.

"I've got to get down through this deck to one of the lines," the workman said.

"There's no lines under this deck."

The workman stood up, holding his flashlight down so that Pete could hardly see his face. "Isn't this O-16?"

"No," Pete said. "O-16 isn't even on this deck."

"My mistake." The workman started to go out, but Pete stopped him at the door.

"Why didn't you turn the lights on?" he asked.

"Oh well . . . I thought they'd bother somebody in the next room."

"There isn't any next room. That's a bathroom." Pete reached over and turned the overhead lights on. The man was tall and thin but his shoulders were wide. The long bill of the swordfisherman's cap he wore threw a dark shadow on his face so that Pete could see only the outlines of high cheekbones, a thin nose, thin lips.

Pete read his name and number on the identification badge and, as soon as the man went out, he called up the security desk. "I'm probably haywire," Pete told them, "but there was a workman in my cabin using nothing but a flashlight and trying to take up a welded deck plate with a monkey wrench. His number was 1753-A and the name on the badge was H. Weber."

"All right, Commander, we'll look into him and call you back."

Pete took a shower and went to bed. The telephone rang and it was Security. "Weber checked out of the East Gate just before we could notify all the gates, Commander."

"He's probably just a sneak thief," Pete said. "I'd watch him though."

"We'll put somebody on him when he comes to work tomorrow."

"Okay," Pete said wearily. "Good night."

Pete was half asleep when he suddenly remembered the log in his desk safe. He flipped on the lights and opened the front of his desk.

The flimsy combination lock on his desk safe had been wrenched almost off and the gray enamel all around the lock was chipped down to bare metal. But the lock still held.

Pete called the O.D. "Got any mechs on duty tonight, Joe?" Pete asked.

"One right here, Captain."

"Send him up to my cabin with whatever he needs to break into my desk safe, will you, please?"

"Coming right up, Captain."

In a few minutes a machinist's mate came up with a bag of tools.

"Somebody tried to break in. One of the yard people," Pete explained. "I want to find out if he got in and then relocked it or whether I came in at the wrong time."

"Doesn't look like he got it open, Captain. But he was sure banging away at it."

The mech prized open the thin steel door. "No, he never got in. See, he broke the tumblers off. He couldn't have locked it again in the shape it's in now, Captain."

"Thanks very much, Larsen."

The mech saluted and went out.

Pete took out the package, unwrapped it, and flipped the pages with his thumb. Then he put it under his pillow and went to bed. Above his bunk, hanging in a shoulder holster, was his issue .38-caliber revolver. He took it out, opened the cylinder, and looked at the six cartridges in it.

Putting the gun back, Pete lay thinking.

Who is Weber? he wondered. Where did he come from? Had he ever been in Cuba?

Was he the "tall one"?

The Purple Heart

In the morning things looked different to Pete. For a long time, while his ship quivered with the hammering going on below, he sat in his cabin staring out the open porthole.

At last everything seemed to fall into line in his mind. All of his plans from now on had to be made to fit around Johnny lying in that hospital.

So Pete made a decision which he had been putting off for a long time. With the war almost over, a few of the Reserve officers would be taken into the Regular Navy. They would never be as real a part of the Navy as the Annapolis officers, but—Johnny needed the money.

Williams knocked and came in. "How was your brother, Pete?"

"Broken back," Pete said. Then he told Bill how it had happened and all the rest. He ended by saying, "So I've changed my mind about staying in the Navy, Bill. I've got to stay in now. I need those blue checks twice a month to keep Johnny in that joint up there."

Williams looked at him. "What about the *Santa Ybel*? I think there's a lot of money in there, Pete. Enough to take care of Johnny."

"And maybe there's none," Pete said.

"My dad will back you. He'll pay for everything you need to go find it. He told me he was so sure about this that he'd put up every cent he had."

Pete shook his head. "It's too risky, Bill. If I didn't find it, where would Johnny be? And your father? Johnny would have to go without the treatment that might cure him. And your father would have lost his shirt."

"My dad has spent his life taking chances," Bill said.

"Not with another man's life, Bill."

"I guess you're right."

"Why don't you go find the *Santa Ybel?* If you found it, you'd get enough money to retire for the rest of your life."

Williams shook his head. "That's the trouble. I don't want to retire. I like to work; I like ships and engines and the sea. If I had a lot of money, I wouldn't be worth putting out with the cat."

"Well, I'll give the log to your father then. He can find somebody to go get it."

"He wouldn't take it as a gift. Maybe you would go in with him as a partner."

"Any way he wants it. . . . Come in," Pete said as someone knocked.

A messenger came in with a sheaf of papers.

Pete glanced at them and held one out to Bill. "The Japs had better start running. Martin's going back to the Pacific," he said.

Bill read Pete's orders in silence and handed them back. "Where are mine, chum?" he asked.

"As soon as I get through my physical exam, I'll go see the admiral about you," Pete said. "Well, wish me luck on my lame arm, will you?"

"They won't even notice it," Williams said.

"Martin, I've got some bad news for you."

Pete, who was tying the black necktie, turned slowly around to face the doctor sitting on the corner of the desk.

"Mind taking your shirt off again and letting

me have a look at that arm, Martin? They've given you a 'down' outside."

"Sir?" Pete said. Then his mouth got dry and he couldn't swallow. When he tried to unbutton his shirt, his fingers felt like rubber balls. He stopped moving for a moment, took a deep breath, and then, steady again, he took off his shirt.

"How much movement have you got?" the doctor asked.

"Plenty, sir. And it never bothers me any more."

"Let me see. Can you reach around behind and touch your shoulder blades?"

"Well, sir, no. But you don't do much reaching back there unless you're in a bathtub."

"Can you touch your shoulder with your fingers?"

Pete tried until the pain in the muscles around his elbow almost made tears come in his eyes. His fingers, reaching, could not touch his shoulder.

"Straighten it right out now," the doctor said.

Pete looked down at his arm, the long scars still bright. It wasn't very straight.

"They did a marvelous job on that arm in Pearl," the doctor said. "I'm surprised that you've got that much movement. But it's no go, Martin. You can't go back out in the Pacific with that arm."

Pete looked straight at him. "Commander, I've

been running a PC around the Gulf for months now," he said slowly. "This arm hasn't bothered me or stopped me from doing whatever I had to do. Couldn't you just give it an okay on the Y sheet and let me go? It means a command to me, sir, in the Pacific."

"I wish I could. Really. But you aren't fit for duty out there."

Pete felt a slow anger. "Commander, I didn't get this arm falling downstairs."

The doctor nodded. "I know it. And I know that a Navy Cross and a Purple Heart don't make up for it either. But look at it this way. You've done a good job. The war'll be over in a month and there are plenty of ships and men to take care of what's left of it. Why not relax and take it easy?"

"What about—the Regular Navy?" Pete asked slowly.

"You mean can you pass a physical for Regular Navy? No. Under the peacetime physical requirements you haven't got a chance, Martin."

"Couldn't I get a waiver? If I gave the Bureau a big story about how I got banged around in combat, wouldn't that help me get a waiver?"

The doctor shook his head. "You might get a little pension out of it. But you'd never get into the Regular Navy with it."

"Well," Pete said, picking up his orders, "I guess I'll go join the feather merchants."

The doctor stood up and held his shirt for him. "I really hate to do this to you, Martin. I've had a lot of people in here faking ailments to keep from going to sea. It hurts to turn down a man who really wants to go."

"Thanks," Pete said.

Out in the sunshine he walked slowly along the graveled path.

What happens to Johnny now? he asked himself. Already there were rumors that the Japanese were asking for peace. Perhaps in only a matter of weeks he would be out of the Navy. And out of a job. Already all his savings had been spent getting Johnny started.

What happens now? Pete asked himself. Then he swung his left arm out, the hand a fist. He looked at it bitterly and put his fist in his pocket.

The *Santa Ybel* was the only answer. If Mr. Williams could take care of Johnny while he outfitted a sailboat and went searching for treasure, he could pay him back—if he found it. If he didn't . . . Well, Pete thought, that comes later.

Aboard ship he asked Bill to come up and, when he shut the door behind him, Pete told him what had happened.

"I think it's a good thing, Pete," Williams said slowly. "You never really wanted to go Regular and you would never have been happy in the peacetime Navy. Look at you now. This is peacetime duty—this yachting around the Gulf. And you've hated every minute of it. So—get your hat, we're going over to Miami to see Dad."

"All right," Pete said. "But before we go, I want to check on that fellow Weber."

He called Security and asked them. Weber had not come to work that morning. He had given as his home address the Regent Hotel.

Pete called the hotel and as he waited Bill said, "What're you going to say if he answers the phone?"

"I'll ask him if he would be interested in contributing ten dollars to the Injured Naval Officers' League."

But there was no Weber registered at the hotel and they could not find any indication that he had been registered there during the past month.

Pete put the phone down. "I'm probably cock-eyed. But I can't get rid of the feeling that that man who wrecked my desk safe is the same one who murdered the Cubans. The 'tall one,' Bill."

"Sounds like it. But how in blue blazes did he find out? How did he know it was in your safe? How did he get here? What is he, a magician? You know, people can't just go and come from Cuba to Key West the way they could before the war."

"Maybe it was this way, Bill. Narvez and his son tried to escape from him by sailing out into that storm. Weber, if that's his name, found out about it and set out after them. He finds them,

68

but he's just a few minutes late, because we're there. He spots us and stays in sight just long enough to read our number. When we leave the wreck, he comes in and finds both bodies gone.

"There're only two things now. Either the log sank or it's aboard my ship. If it sank, it's all over. So Weber comes straight to the Keys. It wouldn't be hard to sneak a small boat in to one of those deserted islands. And Weber has no doubt got all the papers a civilian needs these days—draft card, identification, and all the rest. He finds out where our home port is. That isn't too hard to do."

"You make him out to be a pretty sharp operator," Williams said.

"No, just a man with a very logical mind." Pete suddenly stood up. "I think there's an idea loose in my mind," he said, reaching for the ship's service telephone. "Ask the pharmacist's mate to come up to the captain's cabin," he said.

When the pharmacist's mate came in, Pete smiled at him and waved toward a chair. "This isn't official, and it's off the record, Phillips. I just want to know if you've been on liberty since we made port and, if you have, did you say anything to anyone about the two Cubans we picked up? . . . It's not official and whatever you say is between us."

"Well, sir, I don't think I said anything I shouldn't have said. I met a fellow who said he'd heard about it and thought maybe he knew who the Cubans were."

"What'd he look like?" Pete asked.

"Tall, thin fellow. Had a GI haircut. Thin face. I didn't talk to him much, Captain."

"Did he ask you about the box the Cuban had?"

"Well, he just asked if the old man had any valuables on him. But since I didn't know him, I just said that any personal effects in a case like that were taken in custody by the commanding officer."

"That's all I wanted to know, Phillips. And you handled him exactly right. Thanks very much."

Phillips looked relieved as he got up and went out.

Pete turned slowly toward Williams. "A man with a very logical mind," he said quietly.

"And a good deal more. He's smart, Pete. He thinks fast and straight. I believe we'd better keep remembering that all the time."

"And we'd better get rid of the *Santa Ybel* log," Pete said. "As long as that thing is anywhere he can find it, the whole scheme can blow up in our faces."

"Where're you going to put it?"

Pete sat studying the toes of his shoes on the shelf of his desk. Then he took his feet down. "Doesn't the Navy itself say that the U.S. Post

Office is a pretty secure institution?" Pete got the log, wrapped it carefully in plain brown paper, tied it securely, sealed it, and addressed it to Mr. Pete Martin, c/o General Delivery, Dadesville, Georgia.

"Everybody in Dadesville knows me by sight and Mr. Barney, the postmaster, wouldn't give this to anyone else on earth."

"Okay. Let's go see Dad."

Before they left, Pete folded up an unmarked chart of the Gulf of Mexico and put it into a big manila envelope. Then, down in the ship's post office, Pete asked when the next mail was going out.

"I'm closing the bag right now, Captain."

"Can I throw this in, Stuart?"

"Yes, sir." The yeoman weighed the package, put stamps on, and then canceled them with a United States Navy stamp. Pete watched him toss the log of the *Santa Ybel* into the mail pouch, then draw up the strings, click the lock, and put the wire seal on it.

As Pete and Bill left the ship, Pete said, "If Weber can get the log now, he can have it. I don't want to compete with a man smart enough to figure that one out."

"I believe it's safe, Pete. The only chance of his getting it will be between the time it leaves the ship on the truck and when it reaches the main post office."

"I'll write to Mr. Barney and ask him to let me know if it gets there."

They showed their passes at the gate and walked on toward the town of Key West. It was almost sunset and the old town with its narrow, gloomy streets and Spanish-looking buildings seemed even older than it really was.

On the corner just before they reached the bus station, a gang of kids—about a dozen of them —came down the street led by one who looked to be about twelve years old. They stopped Bill and

Pete and tried to sell them some picture post cards of Key West.

Pete and Bill turned them down, but the kids kept yelling at them and clustering around their legs.

"Listen, shove off, sailors," Pete said.

Then, with no warning, and very swiftly, the biggest of the kids shoved in close to Pete, grabbed the envelope containing the chart, and ran. As he grabbed it, he said in a low voice, "Okay, block 'em."

As Pete lunged after him, he found a solid wall of kids around his legs. He stopped and so did Bill as the kid with the chart disappeared down a narrow alleyway.

"All right, he got away," Pete said to the boys around his legs. "You can let go now. And tell him for me that it was a very nice operation all around."

The kids all ran in a different direction and Pete and Bill walked slowly on.

At last Bill said, "Weber isn't going to like it when he opens that up and finds nothing but an H.O. chart."

"I hope he spends all night going over it with a microscope," Pete said. "Because there isn't a mark on it."

"We learn a little every day, don't we, Skipper? Our little lesson for today is, 'Don't ever mark down the fix you got on the *Santa Ybel.*'

Just keep those little numbers up under your skull. . . . And now here is a minion of the law."

Bill went over to the policeman. He seemed unusually angry and upset as he told the cop what had happened. Pete joined in by saying that the stuff the kid had swiped was official Navy papers. The cop said he would do something about it right away and went off toward the alley.

"Weber is probably watching us out of one of these windows. Oh well, on to Miami. . . . You know, Pete, my dad is going to get a whale of a kick out of this whole thing. He doesn't have much fun sitting in that wheel chair year after year."

"Neither will Johnny, if he can get as far as a wheel chair," Pete said.

Book Two

ESCAPE

Mike

1

In the spring of 1946 a curious craft lay berthed at the yacht club in Miami. In the other berths the sleek yachts, the Sunday sailboats, the cruisers and fast runabouts made the old schooner look even older and more curious than she really was.

Her name was *Indra* and she was exactly forty-six years old. Unlike the other yachts, her standing rigging was thick, heavy stainless steel, the deadeyes tarred, and there were balls of bally-wrinkle on the shrouds to keep the sails from chafing through. Her new canvas was stiff and heavy, her running gear was all stout stuff. Unlike the smart boats around her in the yacht club, she was rigged for the open sea.

From a room in a Miami apartment house Pete Martin, civilian, and a frail, broken man sat looking down at the old schooner. Pete had changed a good deal since he had been released to inactive duty. All the fat which easy living had put on him was gone and he was nothing now but rawhide muscles and bone. His skin, after steady months under the sun, was burned brown, his face was lean with little wrinkles of fatigue showing around his eyes, and his teeth looked very white. His brown hair had been bleached by the sun and he never seemed to have time to get it cut regularly. His hands were rough and calloused; the dungarees he wore almost all the time were threadbare at the knees and elbows and across the back of his shoulders.

The man with him, looking down at the *Indra,* was Wild Bill Williams's father. Mr. Williams had once been a huge man but, after a derrick had collapsed on him during a salvage job in Valparaiso and broken nearly every bone in his body, there was nothing left of him but the broken frame of bones, the skin flabby on it. Only his face, cruelly lined by the permanent pain, seemed to be really alive.

During the months Pete had worked with him, he had found that Mr. Williams was one of the finest people he had ever known, and one of the smartest. Sitting forever in the wheel chair before the window, he seemed able to accomplish almost as much as Pete, who was free to walk the streets and swing a calking hammer.

"She's ready to go," Pete said.

"Looks good. Do you think the hoist on the stern is heavy enough, Pete?" Mr. Williams asked. "After all, the heavy diving suit with you in it will weigh better than three hundred."

"I got some ironwood out of the Everglades. That thing hauled up a dead weight of six hundred pounds," Pete said.

"Good. When do you plan to sail?"

"That's what grinds me," Pete said. "I could sail tonight only I can't get anyone to go along. I've offered as much as a hundred a week but nobody wants it. All the young guys coming out of the service want something permanent. They won't listen to a couple-of-months proposition. And all the old ones are either lousy with dough or they are too lazy to heave on a gaff halyard. And you'd be surprised how many men there are in the world who don't know a lazy jack from a ratline."

"One will show up." Mr. Williams looked out the window at the young people moving around on the docks of the yacht club. "I can't understand it," he said quietly. "Look at all those young men down there. All healthy, all able-bodied. Some of 'em are even sailormen. I think that if I was one of them now I'd pay to go along with you."

"I hate to wait," Pete said. "But maybe in a

week or so I'll find somebody with guts enough to sail outside the breakwater."

"What about Weber?" Mr. Williams asked.

Pete shook his head. "Haven't seen hair nor hide of him. I think he's either lost the trail or given up."

Mr. Williams glanced at him and then turned back to look out the window. "I hope you're right. But I don't think so, Pete. So far Weber has made only one mistake."

"What's that, sir?"

"He's been watching you get ready. I'm sure of that. He can see that the *Indra* is no single-hander. He should have sent one of his men to go along with you. The fact that he hasn't is his mistake. I'm surprised that he's overlooked the opportunity to plant someone right on the *Indra*."

"I never thought of that," Pete admitted. "But perhaps one of the people I turned down was his man."

"Perhaps. . . . Well, I hate to see her lying there when she could be sailing for the two islands, but it can't be helped."

Pete stood up. "I'll discover a sailor somewhere. I'll——"

Before he could finish Wild Bill came in. "Looky, cooky," he said, waving some papers around.

Pete read over Mr. Williams's shoulder Bill's

orders to go as commanding officer of a destroyer escort. Bill was a lieutenant commander now.

"Yak, yak," Pete said. "At last you're going to earn part of your pay."

"Quiet in the civilians," Bill said. "And my beautiful new ship is stationed right here in Miami, Florida, U.S.A. I've ordered me a red-and-green deck chair for watches on the bridge."

Pete snorted.

They congratulated Bill on getting a command and Pete left for the yacht club.

As he walked along the dock Pete felt trapped. In his pocket he had two hundred and fifteen dollars and that was the last of Mr. Williams's money. Everything had cost more than they had thought it would and now he hated to tell Mr. Williams that all the money was gone. What was worse, he had been holding back from the sick man some of Johnny's hospital bills and they were piling up.

If I could just get out of here, he said to himself helplessly. If I could just get down to the islands. Just get under the water.

If I could just get a man with guts enough to go.

Pete thoroughly resented the gaily dressed men on the fancy yachts tied up in the berths. Not a real man in the crowd, he decided. Then as he walked along, scowling, a particularly beautiful yacht caught his eye. She was a tall-masted, black

sloop more than fifty feet on deck. Painted on a
life ring was her name: AUF WIEDERSEHEN. She
was a pretty thing and as trim as a needle. Pete
walked slowly toward her, admiring her lines and
feeling in his bones the way she would go in blue
water. She wasn't a heavy-weather boat but, Pete
thought, she'd be fast as greased lightning in half
a gale.

A man came topside on the sloop and stood
looking out over the stern. He was dressed in
white trousers and a blue blazer and had on one
of those silly caps yachtsmen sometimes wear.
Pete mentally gave him a low grade as he walked
past the bow of the sloop.

Then the man turned around, looking up at
the bare masts of his ship.

When Pete saw his face, he lowered his own
head, turned his face half away, and slouched
on down the dock.

The man on the black sloop was Weber.

Pete walked on past the *Indra* without even
glancing at her and went up the hill to the clubhouse. Going over to the clerk's desk, he leaned
on the rail nonchalantly and remarked, "That
black sloop that just came in is a beauty."

"Sure is. The *Auf Wiedersehen*. What is that,
German?"

Pete nodded. "Means 'I'll be seein' you.'"

"Funny name for a boat."

Auf Wiedersehen. That isn't so funny, Pete

thought. I'm beginning to understand that now.

"Who's the owner?" Pete asked.

The clerk shuffled through some file cards. "Name of Weber. Herman Weber. Jax."

"Don't know him. Well, *auf Wiedersehen*."

The clerk laughed a little.

Pete went into the glass-fronted "deck" and sat down in one of the overstuffed chairs. He could see the masts of the black sloop, see Weber sitting in a deck chair with a chart unrolled in his lap. Two other men, all dressed up, came topside and joined him.

After a while Pete got up and went over to the phone booth. He asked for long distance and put in a call for Lieutenant George Gray, Room 3452 Annex, Navy Department, Washington.

When the phone rang, Pete was waiting.

"Lieutenant Gray? . . . This is Pete Martin, George. In Miami. How are you? Still running the Navy? . . . George, can you help me out? I want to know all you can tell me about a man named Herman Weber . . . yeah, *w*. I think he is, or was, a German. . . . Okay, I'll hang on."

"Pete," George said, and Pete could hear the rustle of papers. "We've got some official stuff on him but here's the public info. At least, this is on *a* 'Herman Weber.' . . ."

"Okay, shoot."

"His name used to be Hermann Webreschacht. Born: Hamburg, Germany, 1911. Joined the

Nazi party in 1932. Attended one of Hitler's schools for junior Fuehrers. Got into some trouble and was thrown out of the party in 1936. Came to the U.S. Apparently had plenty of money and set himself up as a shipbroker and in the export-import business mainly in Cuba and the West Indies. Became a naturalized U.S. citizen in 1941. Then he got into trouble in Cuba. Was accused of assault and battery against a Cuban named Roberto Narvez. He beat the rap, but it made quite a stink at the time."

"Is that all, George?"

"That's all I can tell you, Pete. But if you run into him, it wouldn't do any harm to keep an eye on him. If you know what I mean."

"Thanks, George."

Pete paid for the phone call and left the clubhouse. He went up through the little park so that he wouldn't be seen by Weber and, when he got to the *Indra*, he cast off his mooring lines. Then he sat on deck, looking down the row of boats, until he saw Weber go below on the black sloop.

Keeping the engine at dead slow so that it would make very little noise, Pete backed out of the slip, gave the sloop a wide berth, and slipped on down the bay. As the rows of gently swaying yachts were blotted out at the turn, Pete gave her the gas and fought the incoming tide.

Watching the tide coming in, feeling the fair wind blowing, Pete thought bitterly, If I only had a man to go with me, I could sail tonight. I could get canvas on her and keep going. I could lose that sloop in the darkness and never see Weber's face again.

The feeling of being trapped in the bay grew until Pete almost couldn't stand it. If he could only get out on blue water, he thought.

It was almost sunset when he dropped anchor and let out scope on the anchor chain so that the *Indra* would swing easy with wind and tide. The low sun made huge shadows on the white city, but he was far away from the polish and glitter of the yacht clubs and boulevards. He was down where the tourists don't go—down opposite the ramshackle warehouses and weather-beaten tenements.

It was dark when Pete brought his supper up to the cockpit. He put the plate and cup on the helmsman's seat and ate slowly, not tasting anything except the sugar in the black coffee.

His mind was blank as he took the dishes below and washed them in the galley sink and hung them back in the racks. Then, standing in the gloom of the main cabin, he looked slowly around.

The main cabin, which had been a pleasant "yachty" room when he bought the *Indra*, had been transformed. Pete had taken out the double-deck bunks on one side, the mahogany table in the middle, the fancy lockers and trimmings.

Now, hanging from special racks, and looking like huge ghosts in the gloom, were the two diving suits—one a heavy, deep-water rig, the other a lighter self-contained outfit with an oxygen bottle and caustic soda regenerator. The corselets and helmets, the faceplates, shining a little, were secured on wide shelves. The thirty-two-pound lead shoes were prevented from galloping around in heavy weather by fiddles, and the lead chest and back weights were also secured. On the other side of the cabin the flexible air hoses were coiled down in big loops, and the life line, the telephone cord imbedded inside it, was flemished down. In a special shockproof box Pete had made himself were the two chronometers which, in the silence of the cabin, Pete could hear faintly ticking. His sextant and an octant were in a box on another shelf.

Aside from the diving equipment, there were coils of new hemp rope, spare fittings for almost everything aboard ship, parts and tools for the air pump and ship's engine. Folded and tagged— the storm suit tagged with red labels—were spare sails.

Pete was bitter as he came up into the deep, self-bailing cockpit. The glow from the city of Miami lit the topside of the *Indra* as Pete walked past the big air pump, covered now with heavy tarpaulin. He stopped there a minute, just looking at the thing.

A sound aft interfered with his thinking, and he went back toward the cockpit.

In the pale light from the city he saw a hideous head rising above the scupper rail. The hair on it was long and matted and in the half-light looked like a nest of snakes. The eyes peering out from behind the tangle of hair were sharp and glittered like a rat's.

A body came up with the head and, suddenly, with a heave a small figure rose to its feet on deck.

"Ahoy, mate," a voice said.

Pete walked slowly toward it. "Well?" he said.

"Saw you anchored out here and thought I'd pay you a little visit."

Pete stopped a few feet away and peered down. The thing was either a midget or a small boy. Whatever it was, the last Saturday night bath it had taken had been about 1939, Pete estimated.

"Glad to see you," Pete said. "But I'm busy right now. Come back next week."

"Had chow yet, mate?" the thing inquired.

"All through. So long."

Pete started down the companionway. When he saw that his guest was still standing there, he said, "Good-by. Shove off."

The thing turned and walked slowly back to the rail. Pete saw one leg go over the life line as he went on into the cabin and switched on the lights.

When he turned around, the thing was standing in the cabin doorway.

It wasn't a midget; it was a boy. Under the rat's nest of hair there was a face dirtier than Pete thought a human face could get. Only the bright blue eyes looked clean. The boy was wearing a cast-off khaki shirt, both sleeves torn off at the shoulders and no buttons anywhere. His pants had once belonged to a man who weighed two hundred pounds and were wrapped around the boy and secured with a piece of dirty rope. One leg of the pants had been torn off only a few inches from the ground; the other leg was raggedly torn above the knee. Pete was surprised to see heavy Army shoes at the ends of the legs.

MIKE

The boy looked slowly around the cabin. "What a tub," he said.

"Look, fella," Pete said quietly, "why don't you go crawl back under that rock?"

The boy was looking past Pete into the galley

where Pete's sea stores were held in racks on the bulkheads. "What's chances of a can of beans, mate?" the boy asked.

"None," Pete said. "Shove off."

The boy irritated him, and the smell from his unwashed body was spreading all over the ship.

"So you wouldn't give a friend one can of beans," the boy said.

Pete gritted his teeth and advanced on the boy. "If you don't shove off, you know what I'm going to do? I'm going to take you by the seat of those baggy britches and the back of your neck and drop you in the drink."

"You—and how many Marines?" the boy said.

Pete could stand no more. He reached for the kid, grabbing him by the shoulder.

Afterwards Pete couldn't tell exactly what happened. Something hard, heavy, and moving fast struck him on the shin of his left leg. The pain made him turn the boy loose and grab his leg with both hands. This movement brought his chin down low and something else hit that.

There was an explosion of lights in front of Pete's eyes and a wild singing noise, then all was dark and peaceful.

When Pete came to, he was sitting on the floor slumped against the empty legs of the heavy diving suit. His chin hurt, and his head ached with a slow throb. He slowly put his hand up and discovered a growing lump on his chin.

As the inside of the cabin swung back into focus, he saw something moving. Leaning forward and straining his eyes, he saw the little boy. Under one arm he had a loaf of bread, and in each hand he had a can of beans. He was walking toward the companion door.

Pete was so mad that he was shaking when he got to his feet. The boy stopped, let the loaf of bread fall, and drew back his right arm, the can of beans shining in his hand.

Slowly then Pete began to grin. He thought of himself—a strapping six-footer, a big hero with a Navy Cross—knocked silly by a street urchin.

"Okay," Pete said. "Go heat 'em up in the galley."

The boy relaxed his arm just a little. His eyes watched Pete warily from under the tangle of hair.

"I'm licked," Pete said. "Go heat your beans."

The boy suddenly smiled. Pete was surprised at the shyness of it and at the way the toughness disappeared.

The boy put some coal on the Shipmate stove and put the two cans of beans into a pan of water.

"Don't want you to think I'm stingy," Pete remarked, "but can you eat two cans of beans?"

The boy looked around. "Why not?"

Pete shrugged. "Lots of beans."

The boy pointed at his stomach. "Big hole."

"Go right ahead," Pete said.

The boy picked up the coffeepot and shook it, listening to the coffee sloshing around. "Hah," he said, "Joe."

"What?"

"Jamoke. Java," he said, putting the coffee on the back of the stove. "Gut rust."

"What'd you hit me with?" Pete asked, leaning back against the drainboard.

The boy silently held up his fist and then one foot, shod with the heavy Army shoe.

Pete inspected the fist, then the wrist and arm and shoulder. In the rags and tatters the boy looked small and helpless, but Pete discovered that he had a wide, flat pair of shoulders under the baggy shirt, slim hips, and a boxer's legs.

"How old are you?" Pete asked.

"Let's don't get personal, Mac," the boy said.

"My mistake." Pete looked at the boy's back. "Ever worked around boats?"

The boy swung around. "Listen, nosy, for two lousy cans of beans I don't get grilled, see?"

"You're an unpleasant little citizen," Pete remarked.

The boy's eyes were glittery and hard as he surveyed Pete. "What do you expect for two cans of beans, mate, true confessions?"

"Skip it," Pete said. "I thought perhaps you had the instincts of a human being."

The boy turned back to the stove and poked

his dirty finger down into the water. He flipped
the cans out, opened one of them, and hoisted
himself up on the shelf. Then, carefully, he began eating, pouring the beans out in gobs on slices
of bread. He was making quite a mess of himself and the environs.

Pete got a big spoon out of the drawer and
held it toward him. "New invention," Pete said.

The boy took the spoon. "Oh, a pantywaist,"
he said.

The first can of beans went down with hardly
a swallow, and he opened the second can. In a
very short time he had eaten all the beans and a
loaf of bread. Wiping beans around his face with
the back of his wrist and hand, he got down off
the shelf.

"What time do you eat breakfast, mate?"

Pete looked at him. "Listen, horrible," he said
slowly, "from now on you keep off this boat."

"Some eggs would be good," the boy said. "I
haven't ate a egg in a long time. Eggs, sunny side
up, and bacon—for me."

Then he walked out through the cabin, up the
companionway, and across the deck. Pete went
topside in time to see him rowing away in a boat
which had once been a small crate but now had
enough tar in it to keep it from leaking too badly.

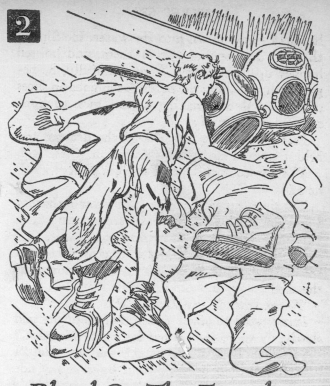

2

Blood On The Faceplate

Pete went ashore early in the morning. As he rowed up to the stinking, dirty wharves, he looked for the excuse of a boat the boy had used but didn't see it. Pete had locked up every hatch and port on the *Indra* and he hoped that the dirty urchin wouldn't break a skylight to get another can of beans.

The first thing he did was call Mr. Williams.

"Weber showed up last night," Pete said.

"Where?"

"Can you see a black sloop about fifty feet long down in the basin?"

"Yes. I see it. Is that Weber's?"

"Yes, sir."

"I'm not surprised, Pete. That's his only play now. Since he hasn't been able to get the log, he can only follow you. What are your plans?"

"I sneaked out last night. He knows I'm gone, but I don't think he knows yet where. I'm way down the bay, anchored in the stream."

"Good work."

"I'm going to scour the beach today and get somebody to go with me if I have to shanghai a man. Then I'll get out of here on the tide tonight."

"Weather's making up . . . but I guess you'd better get out to sea as soon as you can."

"I'm going to. I'll let you know what progress I make."

"Good luck."

Then Pete called up the hospital where John was and sat in the bad-smelling phone booth until he heard Johnny's voice.

"Hello, Jawn. How you coming?"

"Pete? Is that you, Pete? Listen, you know what I can do?"

Johnny's voice sounded very excited and Pete could hear him half laughing.

"What can you do?" Pete asked.

"I can wiggle it, Pete. Honest. I can wiggle it back and forth."

"Wiggle what, Jawn?"

"My thumb. My right thumb. You ought to see it. Just as easy."

Pete didn't know why that hit him so hard. A fourteen-year-old boy could—wiggle his right thumb.

"Good work, Jawn. How're they treating you?"

"Fine! I get sort of tired of all the things they do with me, but I can wiggle my thumb now. So I guess they're all right."

"Stay with 'em, boy."

"When are you going to sail, Pete?"

"Not for a while yet, I guess. Got a few more things to do."

Johnny's voice was suddenly slow. "I wish I was going with you, Pete."

"Next time. Give Maw my love."

"I will. Be careful, Pete. You know why," Johnny said.

It was late in the afternoon when Pete Martin trudged back down to the wharves. He felt tireder than he ever had in his life and completely defeated. He felt angry, too, as he remembered the way men had laughed at him when he had asked them to sign on as a hand aboard the schooner. And he felt sorry for the men who had asked to go because the only ones who had asked were just hulks of men, derelicts, drunks, bums, and drifters who only wanted a place to sleep and something to eat. Pete had listened to them all, but not one of them was able-bodied enough to go to sea.

He called up Mr. Williams from a hash house and told him what had happened.

"Too bad, Pete. But the black sloop is still in her berth. Weber and his men have been gone since noon. . . . Whoa, here they come now. They're getting aboard her. Looks like something has happened to one of them—he's got a bandage on his head and the others are helping him aboard."

"Is it Weber?"

"No, it's one of the others. Anyway, Pete, with this storm making up you might as well sit it out in the bay."

"All right," Pete said. "I'll wait unless Weber makes a move."

Pete went out into the darkness, climbed down to his rowboat, and rowed slowly out toward the *Indra*, his back to her, his eyes looking at the white city.

When he bumped against the *Indra* he turned,

threw the painter around the mainsheet bitt, and swung himself up on deck.

The first thing he saw was the new, bright scar on the mahogany hatch of the companionway. The hasp of the lock had been torn off, and the door lay back, both hinges broken.

On the deck, as Pete ran toward the companionway, were drops of blood.

Pete swung himself down the steep companion ladder and stopped in the doorway of the main cabin.

It looked as though a hurricane had swept through the interior of the boat. Books, charts, instruments littered the deck. All the diving gear had been taken down and thrown to one side. Looking through into the galley and his cabin, he saw that the same thing had happened forward.

Pete flipped on the overhead light and stepped into the cabin. Lying between the two diving suits, which looked almost like the collapsed bodies of men, was another body. Pete recognized the ragged khaki shirt, the baggy pants.

The boy was lying awkwardly, his neck twisted back and his face down on the faceplate of the heavy helmet. In the light Pete saw blood running very slowly across the glass faceplate and on down the polished metal helmet.

Remembering his instructions in the Navy not to move a man if there was any chance that his back had been broken, Pete stooped and felt for the pulse in the limp wrist and then he saw the faceplate cloud with the boy's breathing. Pete moved first one arm and then the other and then the legs. There was no catch in the limp, dead movement. Then, very carefully, he moved the head and at last lifted the boy up, convinced that the backbone and neck were intact, and carried him into his own cabin. There the mattress and bed clothes had been yanked off and thrown on the deck.

Pete put the boy down on the mattress and got a wet cloth from the kitchen. Swabbing back the matted, dirty hair, he saw a very ugly purple welt across the face from the temple down almost to the mouth. The skin had been smashed open at the cheekbone and was still bleeding.

Pete got the first-aid kit and put a sulfa powder dressing on the boy's cheek. He was looking for any other wounds when the boy came to and began to struggle. Pete put his hand on his chest and held him down.

"Take it easy, mate," he said.

The boy raised his head. "Where'd they go?"

"They've gone."

The boy settled back and put his hands to his forehead. He groaned a little and then opened his eyes. "You shoulda been here," he said.

"What happened?"

The boy tried to sit up, and Pete helped him get his back against the solid bunk.

"I thought it was you," the boy said, taking time out to feel around inside his mouth with the end of his tongue. "Thought I'd come out and chat a while. When I got on board, I saw how the hatch had been broken open. So I sneaked down into the cabin, and there were two joes taking the place apart. I went back to the lazaret and got a marlinespike and came back to the cabin.

"They were really wrecking the place. I sneaked along the bulkhead there." The boy pointed into the main cabin. "I let one of them have it with the marlinespike and went for the other one when the first one let out a grunt. I was doing fine until the third one came out of the galley. I only saw him for a second—a tall, skinny drink of water—before he slapped me in the face with a pistol."

"You're going to have a first-class shiner," Pete said. "What did the skinny one look like?"

"I hardly saw his face. I was watching the barrel of that gun." The boy pushed himself up with his hands and got to his feet. He held his head in both hands. "See any cracks in my head?"

"No. Just where he walloped you."

The boy looked out with his good eye from under the tangle of hair. "What were they looking for, mate?"

"For something they'll never find," Pete said

slowly. "Something that is only in my memory."

"Good thing they didn't get in there. Look at the mess!"

Pete sat down on the framework of the bunk and looked into the main cabin.

Weber was closing in on him—fast. Pete knew that his only way of escape was the open sea.

He looked speculatively at the boy. The kid was certainly a scrapper. No one had asked him to take on Weber's gang singlehanded. And under all the dirt and matted hair the kid had intelligence in his eyes. Maybe, Pete thought. It's a long chance but I'm desperate now. I've got to get out on open water.

"How you fixed for beans, mate?" the boy asked.

"Would you settle for a steak dinner?"

The good eye looked suspicious. "Don't kid me, Mac."

Pete looked at him. "Son, I'm in no mood to kid anybody. Come along."

"Where are we going?"

"Ashore," Pete said.

When Pete tied up at the wharf, he told the harbor police what had happened and asked that they keep an eye on his boat for the next few hours. Then he took the boy into the nearest decent steak house. Across the table, with the linen tablecloth, the boy looked very much out of place in his ragged clothes and with the uncut hair. When the waiter came, frowning, Pete gave him fifty cents and ordered two steak dinners. Then he waited until the boy was half through wolfing the food before he said, "How would you like to sail with me?"

"Sail where?"

"Gulf."

"What's in it for me?"

"Maybe a thousand bucks, maybe nothing."

"What's the gag?"

"I need help, that's all," Pete said.

The boy ate two or three huge mouthfuls before he looked at Pete again. "Do you mean that, mate?" he asked, his voice low.

Pete nodded.

"I eat every day?"

"Three times," Pete said.

The boy put his knife and fork down on the clean tablecloth, pushed back his chair, and said, "Let's go."

"Hold hard," Pete said. "What about your parents? Will they let you?"

"I ain't got any parents, Mac. And nobody can tell me whether I can go or not, see?"

"Take it easy," Pete said. "You live somewhere, don't you? You've got some sort of family?"

"I got an old drunk for an uncle. But I don't have to ask him," the boy said. "He'd be glad to get rid of me."

"We'll ask him," Pete said.

The boy's home was the worst hovel Pete had ever been in. A sloppy, unshaven man wearing an undershirt caked with dirt and sweat said he didn't care what the boy did, that he was no good anyway and ought to be in jail. Then the man suddenly said, "You can have him for fifty bucks, mister."

Pete was startled. Then he got mad. "I don't buy people," he said.

"I don't care what you call it," the man said. "But it'll take fifty bucks to get him."

"Don't give it to him," the boy told Pete. "It's a holdup."

Pete ignored the boy and counted out fifty dollars. The man's face fell open with surprise as he took it and shoved it into his pocket.

Outside, walking along, the boy said, "You shouldn't have given him a dime, Mac. The old boozer."

"Never mind," Pete said. Then added, as they came to a neon barber pole, "Next stop."

"What for?"

"You," Pete said.

The boy stepped back. "Let's get this straight, Mac. I don't take any bossing, see? Just like you said, you didn't buy me."

"Maybe not," Pete said. "But you're going in here and you're going right through a Turkish bath, a haircut, and a general overhauling, or we fight it out right here and now."

The boy shrugged. "It's your dough."

"That's right. Now you be here when I get back."

Pete told them in the barbershop what he wanted done to the boy, adding, "And burn every rag he's got on." Then he sent telegrams to Johnny and Mr. Williams. Finally, in an Army-Navy store he spent twenty-two dollars on clothes for the boy: dungarees, sneakers, shirts, and two white outfits. He also bought a comb, brush, toothbrush and paste, and a stack of GI socks.

When he got back to the barbershop, he hardly knew his new shipmate. The boy was standing naked in the rubbing room, scowling, one eye completely closed now and purplish black, the other looking fierce. The barber had cut his hair until no piece of it was more than a quarter inch long and the attendants in the bath had scrubbed him until he was red all over.

"That's the last time I go through that," the boy said.

"First time's always hard. Here, put these on."

The boy's face softened a little when he looked at himself in the mirror. The dungarees were stiff and new, cuffs and shirt sleeves rolled up, but they looked good.

"By the way, what's your name?" Pete asked.

"Mike."

"Ever done any sailboating, Mike?"

"Mine's Pete Martin."

"Okay," the boy said.

No one had been aboard the *Indra* since they had left her; but when Pete and Mike climbed aboard, a harbor police boat came roaring out from the wharves.

"Those dummies," Mike said. "Where were they when we needed 'em?"

Pete proved that he was the owner, and the police went away, leaving him alone on deck with his new hand.

"Ever done any sailboating, Mike?"

"Yeah," Mike said. "I've sailed in everything from shrimpers to lumber boats. I even worked on a yat-chet one summer, but they caught me stealin' the silver spoons and got me thrown in the can."

"The spoons here are aluminum," Pete said.

The boy took a step toward him. "Listen, Mac," he said, "I ain't working for you. You ain't paying me a dime. I'm going along because I want to, see? Why should I swipe your stuff if you ain't even paying me?"

"Good idea," Pete said. "Well, let's go."

"Now?"

Pete nodded.

"In the middle of the night?"

Pete nodded again. "After a while I'll tell you why, Mike."

Mike shrugged. "Suits me, pal."

Clear of the harbor, Pete turned off the engine, and he and Mike got sail on. Back in the cockpit they both sat down, Pete on the wheel.

"This old tub goes pretty good," Mike said. "Right on the wind."

"She's slow, but she's solid as a rock."

They sat in silence for a minute or so. Then Mike drew in a long breath and let it out slowly. "This is okay," he said quietly.

"Yep. Now turn in. I'll rout you out in the morning."

"Don't think I can't handle her, Mac."

"I don't. But I'll take her until daylight."

"Okay, if that's the way you want it."

When Mike had gone below, Pete sat astride the wheelbox. The wind was fitful, sometimes dying so that the sails luffed and slatted. In one of the lulls he stepped over to the hatchway and tapped the face of the barometer. The tendency was still down, the temperature going up, humidity up. It was, Pete finally decided, a bad time to leave port.

Then he looked back at the glow of Miami and scanned the surface of the sea. Nothing appeared on it. The *Indra* had not been followed.

Pete looked up at the sails as they filled with a gust of hot wind. "Let her blow," he said to himself. "There's nothing like a good storm to hide a boat in."

Then he looked back once more across the sea. An icy shiver ran up his spine and tingled in the hair on his neck. The sea was so dark. A black boat could be within five miles of him and he would not be able to see it.

Pete thought of the mess still down in the cabin. The blood on the faceplate would be dry by now.

There was danger in this voyage.

3

The Black Sloop

The wind, which had been rising steadily since three in the morning, died at dawn. Pete, tired and relaxed, looped a leg over the wheel spoke as the sails sagged and slatted. The sun came up into the coppery-red sky and was a huge murky ball of red. Pete looked at it and shook his head. " 'Red sky at night,' " he said to himself, " 'sailors delight. Red at dawning, sailors take warning.' "

The sea became perfectly calm and oily and reflected the redness of the sky until it seemed as though the *Indra* were floating in a sea of blood. Pete left the wheel entirely and pulled the chart board out of the waterproof slide beside the companion hatch. Marking off the last hour's run, he measured the distance back to Miami. Off to starboard he could see a thin pencil line against the horizon made by Elliott Key. He tapped the barometer, and it was still going down.

Pete went back to the wheel. A storm was certainly coming, and he had to make his decision within the hour or it would be too late. To turn tail for Miami meant a beat to windward, and soon he would be too far down to run for shelter behind the keys. It depended, Pete finally realized, on how good a sailor Mike was. Pete had done enough sailing to know that the greatest danger of a storm was not the wind and the sea but the exhaustion of the people handling the boat. As soon as a man got tired, he began making little mistakes; he would keep a sail on too long because he was too tired to want to take it off; he would hold his boat on a squall for a second more than it would take because the effort of shifting sheets was so great to him.

Already Pete had been on the wheel for seven hours and had had no sleep for twenty-four. If Mike turned out to be, at best, a bay sailor, the only thing to do would be to put about and run for Miami.

Ordinarily Pete's seamanship alone would have made him turn and run for shelter. There was no use punishing the boat, and to go back only thirty miles was no loss of distance compared to what he would lose fighting a three- or four-day storm. But Pete kept thinking about the thin man. In the night he had escaped from him; he was free now on the open sea. To go back would put him once more in a position where the man could attack him or at least follow him when he left port again.

It all depended on what sort of sailor Mike was.

Pete hove the *Indra* to and went below to the galley. When he had a huge, hot breakfast ready and coffee simmering on the Shipmate he woke Mike.

"Hit the deck, sailor," Pete said, standing in the door of the little cabin forward of the galley.

Mike scrambled out of his berth almost immediately. "Aye, aye, mate," he said cheerfully. "What's the word on chow?"

"Chow down, but bear a hand."

Pete took his breakfast up to the cockpit and soon Mike, his face actually washed and his hair wet but impossible to comb, came up with a plate heaped to the gunwales.

As he sat down Mike looked around the horizon. "Maybe you wasted money getting my hair cut," he remarked. "Because pretty soon we're going to have a wind that would have blown it right off my head, roots and all."

Pete nodded over the rim of his coffee cup.

"Going back?" Mike asked.

"Don't know. Might," Pete said.

As soon as the sun's rim cleared the sea, the wind began to blow again. Pete noticed that Mike went to the jib sheet without any instructions.

While Mike was up there, Pete took time to glance across the compass card. When Mike came back, Pete gave him a course to steer which was a little too far off the wind for the way the sails were set. Mike climbed up on the wheelbox, still eating, and settled down, steering with one hand and one bare foot, eating with the other hand. Pete, trying not to let Mike see him, watched the compass as it swung over and steadied on course.

Pete almost held his breath as he waited. If Mike went on sailing without suggesting letting the sails out a touch more, then he wasn't good enough on the helm to risk putting the *Indra* through the coming storm. They would have to turn back to Miami—and the thin man would be waiting for them there.

Mike continued nonchalantly to sail and eat, and Pete felt a wave of disappointment rising. He hated to go back. Now that he had escaped to the open sea the thought of going back where Weber was was almost like going into a pit of snakes. But Mike was apparently paying no attention to the set of the sails.

Then Mike, with his face full, mumbled, "How's about letting her out a little, Mac? Might as well get all we can out of the old tub before we get knocked silly."

Pete sighed and grinned. Mike was a sailor.

"Put her over on 197 and let's haul," Pete said. "I want to get away from your pals."

"You mean that narrow drink of water?" Mike asked, spinning the wheel over. "He's no pal of mine, Mac. If I ever see him again, I'll break his head."

"We'll never see him. Not where we're going," Pete said.

"Where *are* we going?" Mike asked. "All that diving gear looks like sponge fishing, but you ain't no Greek from Tarpon Springs."

"I'll tell you later. Keep her as close to 197 as you can and give me a buzz if you need any help. There's a buzzer right under the wheel shaft."

"Okay, I got her."

Pete grinned. "Good."

For a little while after he got into his bunk, he worried about Mike, imagining all sorts of mistakes the kid could make up there. But very soon he was fast asleep.

Pete woke up, looked at his watch, and came

vaulting out of the bunk. With nothing on but his skivvy pants he raced through the littered cabin and up the companionway.

Mike was sitting on the wheelbox steering with both bare feet. The wind was strong and gusty but Mike seemed perfectly calm as the *Indra* bucketed along, gray water swirling in and out of the lee scupper.

"I'm sorry, Mike. Didn't mean to sleep so long. Why didn't you buzz me?"

"If I'd needed you, I'd've buzzed you, Mac,"

Mike told him. Pete got his clothes on and came back. "How are you at cooking?" he asked as he relieved Mike at the wheel.

Mike looked at him. "I'm the best," he said. "I can make a rich soup out of bones a dog wouldn't bury."

"No use straining yourself," Pete said. "But we'd better eat now before it gets too rough to cook."

In half an hour Mike was back with dinner. He had soup, potatoes, string beans, pork chops with onions, and bread. "Anything left?" Pete asked.

"Turnips," Mike said.

As they ate Pete watched some porpoises playing around the bow of the *Indra*. The taffrail log was clicking over fast and occasionally they had to duck spray curling over the weather bow.

"This would be fun if we didn't know what was coming," Mike remarked. "How hard do you think it's going to blow?"

"Hard," Pete said. "You'd better turn in— we'll both be up all night."

The afternoon passed, the wind growing stronger all the time. It seemed to drain the dark blue color out of the Gulf Stream and to leave it a dirty, foaming gray. Around five o'clock Mike came back into the cockpit.

"We'll shorten sail in a little while," Pete said when he saw Mike look up at the spread of fair-weather canvas. "But I want to put as many miles as I can between us and that buzzard."

Mike glanced at Pete. "What's the pitch, Mac?"

Pete told him the story of rescuing the Cuban and the log of the *Santa Ybel*. "I know where it is," he ended.

"What about old Skinny? Does he know too?"

"He knows that the *Santa Ybel* went down with a holdful of gold, but doesn't know exactly where. If he did, he wouldn't be trying to steal the log from me."

"So he'll follow us?" Mike said.

"Yep. But he won't find us. This is a big area."

"Has he got a boat?"

Pete nodded. "A black sloop. Looks seaworthy and fast. Marconi rigged. One of those racing jobs."

Mike said slowly, "A piece of gold as big as an oxcart wheel. How much is that in money, mate?"

"I don't know. But it ought to be worth a lot to a museum."

"You mean we don't melt her down and get some dough for it?"

"A museum'll buy it. There's a lot of other stuff." Pete grinned at him. "Don't worry, fish-face. If we get it, we won't have to bother with digging up dog bones for soup any more."

"I don't much care one way or the other," Mike said. "As long as the food holds out. I haven't eaten this regular since they let me out of school."

"Where'd you go to school?" Pete asked.

"I went to a little institution called a reform school," Mike said.

"Oh."

"Yeah, 'Oh.' I learned a lot of things in that joint, Mac. I learned how to control a honest pair of dice. I learned how to change the numbers on automobile engines and pick ignition locks. I learned some reading and writing too. But I was only in for a year."

"What they put you in for?" Pete asked.

"I just happened to be in a grocery store when the cops busted in the front door. The other guy with me was a fat slouch and got stuck in the window going out."

"Too bad."

"I didn't mind it," Mike said. "We ate good up at school, and I didn't take much of a kicking around."

"How old are you, Mike?" Pete asked.

"Fifteen or sixteen, I guess. Anyway, old enough to know better than crash a store with another fat guy."

A squall whistled down the deck, and Pete eased her. "We'll shorten sail when this one dies," he yelled to Mike.

As the wind died, Pete started forward but

Mike yelled something and he stopped. Mike was pointing back into the gray sky.

Pete looked aft. Against the wall of sea and sky the triangle of a tall sail stood out white and almost glistening.

Without saying anything Pete got the long 8 × 50 binoculars out of the watertight case and turned them on the sail. Slowly he moved the glasses down the long, slim mast until, as the hull of the boat was lifted up by a roller, he could see her black paint shining with water. Pete put the binoculars down, unwrapping the strap from his wrist.

"Is it?" Mike asked.

Pete nodded.

"That skinny drink of water is a smart sailor," Mike said.

"No. I'm a dumb one," Pete said bitterly. "I came right down the groove on the Havana course."

"Well, what do we do?" Mike asked. "That boat he's got can sail circles around this one."

Pete nodded in agreement. "Except—I think we can crack on harder in heavy weather than he can. . . . Let's find out."

"You going to leave this canvas on?" Mike asked, his voice low.

Pete nodded. "And fly some more. We'll put the topsails on her."

Mike looked at him dubiously. "We won't

look so good when the masts blow out," he said.

"That's a chance we'll have to take. If we can outrun him until dark we can lose him during the night. If we don't . . . we'll have to sail around and around until we do, and we can't, Mike— there isn't that much time."

"Hold your hat," Mike said.

A rain squall swept them as they got the top-sails rigged and let them break out of the small stuff lashings. The *Indra* reeled under the impact of the wind in the high sails, and Pete had to ease her off as the lee rail sizzled under the water and waves swirled around the cabin house.

Mike wrapped a hand in the glasses loop and looked back as the rain cleared. "Still coming," he said.

"What's he got on it?" Pete asked.

"Jib, flying jib, and main."

"Watch him for a while and see how he's doing."

The *Indra*, her expanse of sail filled and driving, tore into the seas. The dolphin striker plunged down deep, burying the outboard bowsprit, and when she struggled up Pete could see the triatics go taut as bowstrings. He hated to drive her this way and waited for Mike to tell him whether he was gaining or losing.

Then Mike said, "Oh, oh. He's breaking out a club topsail, mate."

Pete's heart sank as he turned his head for a

moment to see the topsail fill out like a huge balloon on the mast of the sloop.

Then Mike chuckled. "Can't take it. He's furling the flying jib." Mike wiped spray off the binocular lenses and looked again. "Mate, we might as well furl 'em," Mike said slowly. "He's breaking out a balloon jib on us. He'll be alongside in about ten minutes."

"Pray for that storm," Pete said. "Go stick a knife in the mainmast, Mike."

Mike looked at him. "Are you crazy? I wouldn't do that even in a dead calm. What do you want, a hurricane?"

"I could use a piece of one," Pete said. "Let me see."

Pete looked aft with the glasses, and the image leaping at him made him draw in his breath. The sloop had gained a mile on them since they had flown the topsails. The whole front of the sloop was hidden behind the tremendous canvas wall the balloon jib formed and all Pete could see was the welter of white water as the boat drove toward them.

He handed the glasses back to Mike. Spray was coming in flying sheets, and he licked the salt water off his lips and squinted his eyes against it. All around the horizon now the sky was right down on the sea like a gray wall, the wind was whining like a pack of dogs in the stainless rigging and, below the topside sounds, Pete could hear the old *Indra* complaining in her wooden bones.

Pete's body was tense as it swayed and jerked to the rough movement of the pounding ship. With every muscle he was trying to help the *Indra*.

"How're we doing?" he yelled.

"Standing still," Mike yelled back. "He's gaining fast. I can see people aboard her now. Three of 'em anyway."

Pete would not look back as he kept on driving his ship. A sword blade of black cloud swung away from the wall of the sky and curved toward the two racing boats. In the driving wind Pete could feel the heavier wind coming, and he braced himself, wondering if the *Indra* could take it when it got there.

The wind struck like a sledge hammer. The fore-topsail on the *Indra* blew out with a crack like a cannon shot, and the shreds of sail flew straight out and almost stiff in the screaming wind. Waves, gray and racing, foam blowing horizontally off the tops of them, mauled the ship and buried her in foaming water. The bow of the *Indra*, going down like an express elevator from the top of the crests, would drive hard into the body of the next wave and then rear like a wild horse, throwing solid water back the entire length of the ship.

Pete clung to the wheel, gasping for breath and

trying to look up at the straining canvas. The walls of water were breaking against him, almost tearing him away from the wheel, but he did not ease her.

Then Pete felt Mike's hands on him and looked down. Mike was passing a half-inch rope around his waist and making it fast to a bitt. Afterward Mike tied a rope around his own waist.

Then the rain came. Pete had never felt rain like that before even in the typhoons off the Philippines. It didn't fall, it was driven straight across the sea by the wind and had the force of bird shot. It was impossible to keep his eyes open, or even keep his head up against it, but he never eased her, sailing by the feel of the deck under his bare feet and the wheel against his hands and arms.

Th squall died almost as fast as it had started. The rain dribbled away and they were suddenly back in the dim, darkening world.

Mike wiped off the binoculars and looked aft. Then he slumped down beside Pete.

"They look like an old-rags-and-bottles man," Mike said, relief in his voice. "They're bare-poled except for tatters."

Pete looked back and then swung the *Indra* up into the wind. "Take her," he said. "We'll reef her down."

In half an hour they had a triple reef in the main, double in the fore, and a storm jib of heavy canvas forward. The *Indra* seemed to sigh with relief as Pete swung her about and the shortened sail filled with the heavy wind.

Pete turned on the binnacle light as darkness came down like a blanket and then sat looking at the dim yellow face of the compass while Mike steered.

"We're in a bight," he said to Mike. "I'd like to make a 90-degree change of course and really foul them up, but we need sea room too badly. I don't want to wake up in the morning with Cuban palm trees leaning in the portholes."

"How about beating her up as long as we can? That's the last thing they'd think we'd do in weather like this."

"Good idea, Mike. I'd much rather have those jokers in front of us than behind us."

All night long, as the storm gathered its strength, Pete and Mike nursed the *Indra* on the beat to windward. It was hard, nerve-racking work. The black squalls struck them without warning, whirling down out of the black night, and many times they thought a mast was coming out before they could get the bow up into the squall.

Dawn wasn't much different from night and it was eight in the morning before they could call it day, for the sky was gray-black with cloud, rain squalls swept at intervals across the sea, there was only a gloomy light from the sun.

Pete, his eyes burned red with salt and lack of sleep, protected the chart from spray as he walked the dividers on it. Then he shoved it back into the waterproof slide and came to sit down beside Mike.

"If they kept on the same course they were on, they're thirty miles away and to port of us and getting farther away all the time. If we don't see them by noon, I think we can count 'em as lost."

"They couldn't see us in this stuff more'n half a mile—less than that," Mike said.

Pete looked out at the world which seemed to have closed in in a gray ring right around the *Indra*.

He grinned slowly. "That squall saved us."

Mike laughed, salt water running into his mouth. "There wasn't a sail flying on that sloop." Then he looked at Pete. "This is a pretty good old tub," he said.

Pete nodded. "I'm glad to get rid of that bird," he said slowly.

4

Trapped

The storm howled on. Pete,
using the radio compass to get
an accurate record of where he
was in the wild ocean, kept the *Indra* going east
for sea room all morning. She was reefed all the
way down with a small storm jib forward so that
she made little headway. On the other hand, the
shortened sail did not put much strain on her,
and she rode nearly upright except in the hard,
hammering squalls.

124

It was miserable work for the helmsman. Pete, in foul-weather gear—breeches, coat, sou'wester, and rubber boots—was still wet through to the skin. Although the pounding of the *Indra* when they were cracking on had now stopped, a lot of water was still being whipped by the wind from the bows straight aft so that Pete was continually lashed by it. In addition to this, the frequent hard squalls brought a deluge of cold rain to plague him.

The world around him was a gray mess. In that shallow water the waves were enormous and seemed to fence him in with roaring walls which, when one careened, its top sizzling, past the boat, another instantly reared up to take its place. The *Indra*'s motion in the sea was sickening and violent. She would go straight up, on an even keel, as though something had exploded under her and then, as the wave ran out from under her, she would drop with a sick, twisting motion and crash into the trough. Or she would stagger up, her bow in the sky, and then tremble and writhe until her bow suddenly rocked straight down and she slid with awful speed down the front of a fast-moving wave. Or she would do it all backward. She rolled until Pete sometimes thought she was going over. She rolled until the cabin house sizzled with water around the skylights and dripped water below. She rolled until the crosstrees dipped into the sea. Pete, lashed to the ship with a line, steered her with his feet braced against the wheelbox, his knees clamping it as he would clamp a bucking horse.

In the middle of all this, Mike came staggering up the companion ladder, falling from side to side, balancing on each step and bracing himself with knees and elbows. In each hand he had an enormous sandwich.

He lurched across the cockpit and fell, sitting, beside Pete.

He held up one of the sandwiches. "Here," he said.

Pete looked at the thing, the bread already damp with spray, the insides of the sandwich leaking and dripping and squeezing out.

"No, thanks," Pete said. Inside his mouth there was a sudden gush of cold liquid, and his stomach seemed to rise up and then fall slowly over backward and slither down again. When Mike withdrew the sandwich, Pete felt a little better. But when Mike took a huge bite of his own, a bite which caused the red and yellow and gray inside of the sandwich to ooze out, Pete had to look up at the topmast as his stomach did another slow roll.

"You'd better take those things below before Dagwood sees them," Pete decided.

Mike looked up at him, shreds of sandwich from ear to ear. "Thought you were a big strong Navy man."

"Naval Reserve, son. Take 'em below."

Mike got up reluctantly and started below. Halfway across the cockpit he turned. "When I come back, I'll tell you something funny," he said. "It's about a man who tied an oyster to a string and swallowed it and then pulled it up again."

"*Go below!*" Pete yelled.

Mike, laughing like an idiot, staggered back down the companion ladder.

Pete's stomach settled down again, and the wild gushing in his mouth stopped. At the end of the hour he pulled in the counter of the taffrail log and took the hourly reading. As he entered it in the log, he saw that, even under storm canvas, the *Indra* was making three knots. In two more hours, Pete figured, he would have enough sea room for three more days of the battering wind, and he knew that very few storms in that area lasted for more than four days. As he sat down again, he felt suddenly contented and happy.

He thought of the man and the black sloop. Weber had been completely eluded, Pete decided. He was now, probably, sailing all over the Gulf looking for the *Indra*, but his chances of just stumbling on her were very remote.

Pete thought of the squall which had saved them and smiled, salt water running into his mouth. He looked forward along his ship as she staggered up the back of a wave, and a warm feeling of pride rose in him. Maybe she was what Mike called her, "an old tub," but she had certainly outfought and outsailed the slick sloop. The old tub was a seagoing ship, Pete decided, and could take it. And he was glad that he had spent the extra money to put the heavy rigging on her. If he hadn't, he thought, when that squall banged them, the *Indra* would have come up with her masts out—just slopping around helplessly and at the mercy of Weber and his gang of hoodlums.

With the ship moving violently but steadily and without too much strain, Pete had time to do a little sober thinking. What did Weber plan to do? he asked himself. Because he was sure that Weber had not given up and he was equally sure that Weber was an intelligent enemy. Pete had learned a bitter lesson in the Navy—don't underestimate your opponent—so he concentrated on Weber now.

Pete alone knew exactly where the *Santa Ybel* lay. He was sure of that. Narvez knew approximately but, if Pete interpreted the things Weber had done so far, Narvez had not told Weber, and Weber had not actually read the log of the *Santa Ybel*.

Pete put himself in the foreigner's place. What would he do if he wanted to find the *Santa Ybel*?

The answer was simple: Follow the *Indra*.

Then what?

Weber had already searched the *Indra* and had

not found the log of the *Santa Ybel*. Pete was sure that, after he had knocked Mike out with the pistol barrel, Weber had continued his search until he had satisfied himself that the log was not aboard.

If that was right, Pete decided, then Weber would just be cutting his own throat to get tough. If, by a lucky fluke, Weber found the *Indra* again, the only thing he could do would be follow her. It would be useless for Weber to attack the *Indra*. Therefore, Pete figured, he and Mike were safe from any more physical violence until *after* they reached the *Santa Ybel*.

That "after" worried Pete. Once he gave away the position of the treasure ship, he and Mike could stand by for anything. Pete did not for a moment try to kid himself into thinking that Weber would hesitate to do *anything* to get that gold. The man had committed cold-blooded murder in the past.

So the answer was again simple: Weber must never find the *Indra* anchored above the *Santa Ybel*.

That answer made Pete change his plans. Originally, before he had begun to realize how deadly a threat Weber was, he had planned simply to sail down to where the *Santa Ybel* was, anchor there, and dive for treasure whenever the weather was calm enough. And, when the weather was too rough for diving, just lie at anchor.

Pete threw all that out. With Weber in the same ocean, every minute that he stayed anchored above the *Santa Ybel* was going to be dangerous. Instead he would have to pick his days with the greatest care, sail to the spot as fast as he could, dive for a little while, and then get well away from the *Santa Ybel*. That way, Pete figured, narrowed the time of danger, made less the interval when Weber could find him.

Then Pete grinned. He had lost Weber once already. Every minute, every mile the *Indra* sailed in the gray world, widened the area Weber had to search. From Miami, going south, it had been fairly easy for Weber to find him. It didn't take a mental giant to figure that a sailboat, making six knots, would have to be somewhere between Florida and the Bahamas and, as time passed, between the Keys and the Andros. But soon—in an hour—Pete would be turning west into the ninety-mile-wide Straits of Florida. If he could get through them without being discovered, Weber would have to search the entire Gulf of Mexico to find him.

As the *Indra* was carried up to the top of a huge wave, he looked around. He couldn't see a half mile in any direction. The wall of cloud was pressing in close and was lying right down on the wild sea. The wind was full of mist and spray, and the sunlight was shut out so well that, at high noon, it seemed to be twilight.

"Boy," Pete said, "you couldn't find the continent of North America in this soup."

And by nightfall he would be plunging into the immense emptiness of the Gulf of Mexico.

"Good-by, Weber," Pete said. "It was nice knowing you."

Mike came topside and took the wheel when Pete at last turned her west. The motion of the ship eased a little as she began to run, and they took off everything but the storm jib, which they boomed out. The storm was so great that they continued to make three knots under the jib alone.

Pete, down in the cabin, continued cleaning up the mess Weber and his men had made of things. Mike had done a lot but had left the diving gear for Pete. He hung the stuff back on the bulkheads, lashed down the helmets and corselets more securely, flemished down the life line, and coiled the hoses. In his own cabin and Mike's he got things shipshape again and, by the time he was through, he began to feel hungry.

In the galley Pete made himself a sandwich and then, in some doubt, made one for Mike. Eating his as he went up the ladder, he held out the other one to Mike.

"Thanks," Mike said, and began gobbling.

"What was that you were going to tell me about the man with an oyster on a string, Mike?"

Mike grinned, his mouth full. "Forget it, Mac. It didn't work."

"It almost did. Think I'll turn in for a little while." Pete looked at his watch. "Eight bells. How about staying with her until eleven or twelve, Mike?"

"I slept most of the morning. I'll keep her until later if you want."

"We'd better steady down on four," Pete said. "We've got a long time yet."

"Okay. Call you at eight bells."

"Don't forget that oyster if it gets any rougher," Pete said, going down the ladder.

It was pitch-black dark and the buzzer was going like an angry hive of hornets. Pete struggled up out of his bunk and as the buzzer continued to ring without stopping he began to get mad at Mike. "Okay. *Okay!*" he yelled above the noise of the laboring ship.

As Pete ran out through the main cabin, he saw light flickering from topside and for an instant thought that the ship was on fire. But then he remembered how wet everything was up there. As he went up the ladder three steps at a time, he wondered if Weber had, by some freak of chance, found them again.

The whole topside of the *Indra* was lit up with a cold, flickering, wavery light. In it he could see

Mike almost cowering at the wheel, his eyes wide open with fear.

Pete stopped in the companionway and glanced up at the tops of the masts. Then he began to laugh.

Mike straightened up and looked at him.

Pete went on laughing, as he braced himself in the hatch to keep from being thrown back down the ladder.

"Thought you were a sailor," Pete taunted him.

Mike's eyes narrowed. Very deliberately he put a becket on the wheel, got down off the wheelbox, and, with what dignity he could manage on the writhing ship, walked over to confront Pete.

"What are you laughing about, clown?" Mike asked, and his jaw began to stick out.

Pete just laughed.

"Do you want a swat in the teeth, clothhead?" Mike demanded.

"Take it easy, son," Pete said, still chuckling. "But you looked pretty funny squatting back there."

"Funny?" Mike spat the word out. "What's so funny?"

"You," Pete said.

Mike turned and stalked back to the wheel. As he got back on the box and took the becket off, he said, "Here I am sailing around with a clown."

Then the light blazed up bright again, streaming in cold fire up and down the steel shrouds and dancing along the masts and the wire rope edges of the sails.

"Cut the comedy," Mike said, and there was a faint tone of pleading in his voice. "What is that stuff, mate?"

Pete came over and sat down beside him. "St. Elmo's fire. It's good stuff, Mike. The old sailors used to think that it was St. Erasmus coming down to look out for them because you very rarely see it except in storms."

"Doesn't burn?"

"No. It streams down from those two bright spots like fans on the mastheads."

Mike laughed—a little. "Scared the pants off me. I was just sitting here, and all of a sudden those two spots jumped down on top of the masts and began to spit and fizzle like a cat fight. Then all that stuff began to run up and down. Listen to it crackling."

"I remember once when I was in a destroyer," Pete said. "We were sneaking up on one of the Jap-held islands—had a bunch of UDTs to put overside—and it was blowing about like this——"

"Who are UDTs when they're home?" Mike asked.

"Underwater demolition teams—very tough people. Anyway, everything was going fine and we were getting in right on top of the beach when—whammy—all of a sudden St. Elmo's fire lit up the whole ship. We looked like a Christmas tree out there, and in about three seconds the Japoons opened up with everything they had. Felt like those clay ducks in a shooting gallery. And, since we didn't want the Japs to know a U.S. ship was even in that ocean, we couldn't fire a shot. All we could do was back gracefully out of there, still lit up like the Fourth of July."

"What'd you do?"

"Waited until the stuff went away and went back. But it was a nervous bunch of boys on the way back. All hands kept looking up at the masts expecting that stuff to break out again."

"What happened then?"

"Why, son," Pete said, getting up, "we won the war."

"Yeah?" Mike said. "Don't you know who won the war, Mac?"

"No, who did?"

"The United States Marine Band," Mike said.

"That's right, I'd forgotten. . . . Well, good night. Give me a buzz if anything happens—that is, anything important."

"Listen . . ." Mike said, half rising from his seat.

Pete laughed and went down the ladder.

Pete relieved Mike at the wheel at midnight. The storm was reaching its peak, and by three o'clock in the morning it was too rough to handle any longer. Regretfully Pete put enough canvas on the mainmast to heave her to nicely and then just sat there. He hated to lose ground, to have to let the ship be driven backward a mile or so every hour, but the wind and sea were too violent to keep on running. The danger of a jibe was too great even under the short canvas and, in the confused sea, the danger of a wave crashing down from astern and breaking the *Indra's* back grew with the storm.

The *Indra* was a good ship and hove to like a duck. While the storm screamed and roared around her, she seemed to ignore it as she rose and fell with the waves. Pete stayed in the cockpit in case a freak wave should threaten to broach her and listened to the voices you can hear in a real gale at sea. He listened to the voices singing like a great choir of people far away, a choir with each section of voices singing a different tune. To pass the time and keep himself awake, he also studied the waves which came rushing up out of the blackness to become gray-black walls towering all the way into the sky. Each one seemed to be trying desperately to crash down upon the *Indra,* but she ignored them as their white crests began to become visible and then, from the black sky, came roaring down. Every seventh wave, Pete thought, seemed to be bigger than the other six. Number one and number six waves were the smallest.

Around seven in the morning Pete went forward and tightened up the lashings on the dinghy and the fourteen-foot tender, and at eight he buzzed for Mike and asked him to get up some chow.

By eleven the back of the storm was broken, and they got under way again. Pete took the wheel after lunch, and Mike turned in.

By five o'clock in the afternoon the radio compass gave Pete a position almost clear of the Florida Keys. When Mike came on deck, Pete said, "We're almost in the Gulf. I'm going to take my first real breath when we get in it."

"Do you think old Narrow Face is still looking for us?"

"I'm sure of it. And I want him to have a lot more area to search than the Straits."

"Wish I'd seen him coming out of the galley," Mike said. "I'd have let him have it with that marlinespike right between his little peepers."

"I wouldn't care if I never saw him again," Pete declared.

Mike settled down in the cockpit. "Wind's shifting," he said, turning his cheek from side to side. "She'll go around 180 and then die."

Pete nodded. "I hope this sky stays down until dark, though. One more night's run and he'll never find us."

But the sky didn't. Slowly the clouds receded, the wind seemed to push them back, and the small

137

circle in which the *Indra* seemed to have been sailing steadily widened.

Mike took the wheel and Pete went over to the chart board. He was marking in the afternoon DR position when he heard Mike say in a low voice, "Look."

Pete turned slowly around and looked aft.

About a mile away, just emerging from the wall of cloud and sea, was the black sloop, its sails ghostly white.

Pete felt his knees turning to water, and he leaned back against the chart board. On the sloop, standing in the bow, was the figure of a tall, thin man.

Pete slowly lowered his eyes and looked at Mike. The boy was looking up at him, his eyes steady.

"How did he do it?" Mike asked slowly.

Pete shook his head. "I don't know. But he did it."

Mike turned slowly and looked back at the sloop. "What do we do now?"

Pete walked slowly over and sat down beside Mike. "How did he do it?" Pete said, his voice almost a whisper. "In all the thousands of square miles he had to search, how did he find us? In the storm, in visibility less than five hundred yards, how did he get right on our stern?"

Suddenly Pete yanked open the compartment where the long binoculars were kept. He unconsciously and from long training in the Navy wrapped the neck strap around his wrist before he brought the glasses up.

Then, for a long time, Pete stood going over every inch of the black sloop with the glasses. At last he lowered them.

"That's how he did it," he said.

"How?" Mike asked.

"Radar," Pete said.

5

Phantom

"Radar?" Mike asked. "You mean that stuff can see right through a fog?"

Pete sat down, his back to the black sloop. He put his elbows on his knees and held his face in his hands. "Yeah."

"Then he's just been following us wherever we went?"

Pete nodded. "I thought I was being so smart,"

he said bitterly. "And he's been sitting there looking at us on the scope."

Pete slowly straightened up and looked aft. As
he did, the jib of the black sloop luffed and slowly
the boat lost speed and the clouds began to close in
upon her again. At first wisps of clouds drifted
around her and then, as her outline grew wavery
and her white sails grew gray, the black sloop
vanished again into the cloud.

"Can he see us now?" Mike asked.

"Perfectly," Pete said. "We're a pretty little
green line."

"How does that stuff work?"

"It isn't stuff, it's a thing," Pete said. "I don't
know much about it except that it's a cathode-
ray tube and a radio receiver and transmitter.
The transmitter sends out a radio pulse which
lasts about a millionth of a second. If the pulse
doesn't hit anything, nothing shows on the tube,
but if it does hit something, it bounces back.
Since radio waves travel at the same speed as that
of light—I think it's 186,000 miles per second or
minute or something—the radar has a gimmick
that can measure how long it took the pulse to
get there and how long it took the reflection to
get back, so you can read right off the cathode-
ray tube the distance the thing is away from you.
That's where 'radar' came from—'radio detec-
ting and ranging.' Of course the thing sends out
millions of those pulses, not just one, but it

doesn't send out another one until the reflection comes back or just peters out."

"Can he see us all the time then? Can he see us moving around and steering and all?"

"No, it's not that good. All he sees is a wavery green line on a dark round glass thing—the business end of the cathode-ray tube—they call it a 'pip.'"

"Can it go right through mountains and houses and things?"

"Oh no. It can't go through anything but air. But it goes right through fog or rain or darkness."

"H'mmm," Mike said. "We could really use a good-sized mountain right back there, couldn't we?"

Pete turned and looked back at the now blank wall of cloud. As he looked and saw nothing, a feeling of helplessness gripped him; a feeling of being trapped. Weber, with a faster, more easily handled boat, could always outsail him except in very heavy weather. And as long as the *Indra* was within twenty or thirty miles of the sloop, Weber could see it with the radar. Pete suddenly remembered once, in a laboratory, watching some rats in a glass cage.

He began to beat on his forehead with his right fist. Could he jam the radar the way the British jammed the Nazi Würzburg system? No. He had no transmitter. Could he run back to the Keys and count on their obscuring the *Indra* on

the scope? No. They weren't high enough. Could
he, somehow, destroy the radar set on the sloop?
Down in the cabin Pete had an M-1 carbine. But
the sloop would have to come within three hundred yards before he could hope to hit the radar
antenna on the mast. And even if he could hit it,
it would be easy to fix. And Pete didn't want to
start the shooting.

There was nothing he could do. In a little dark
room somewhere on the black sloop the cathode-
ray tube glowed faintly—glowed like the eye of
evil—and the *Indra,* a green line, was always on it.

"Why don't we just call it a day?" Mike asked.
"If that bird brain can follow us with the gadget
everywhere we go, he's got us licked. Just as soon
as we get to the *Santa Ybel* all he's got to do is
come alongside and swarm on us. You got anything that'll shoot?"

"Only a carbine," Pete said.

"One of those toy guns?"

"Not exactly, but it's no cannon."

"Well, let's go back to Miami and go into the
cupcake business. You don't need that gold wheel
anyway; you got plenty of dough."

Pete looked at him somberly. "You know
something, Mike? I've got a brother about your
age. You know what he can do?"

Mike looked curiously at Pete. "No, what can
he do, Mac?"

"He can wiggle his right thumb. And—that's

all he can do. He's lying up in a hospital paralyzed from the neck down."

Mike frowned. "You mean just a kid my age?"

"Yeah. And I haven't got any money, Mike. I've got a little in my pocket. I owe a whale of a lot and I've got to keep Johnny in the hospital. If we don't get that stuff out of the *Santa Ybel*, it'll be the end of Johnny—and me."

Mike turned slowly and, in a low voice, began to curse the thin man. He raised his fist and shook it at the blank wall of cloud. Then he stopped and looked at Pete. "Are those pulses or whatever you called 'em coming right out of those clouds, right now?"

Pete nodded.

"Isn't there some way you can cut 'em off?"

"If I had a high-frequency resnatron tube putting out about 50,000 watts, I could give him a headache. Only it takes seven eight-wheel trucks just to carry it around."

"Then what are we going to do?"

Pete shrugged and slowly stood up. "We might as well eat something."

"Why don't we heave to and both of us cook?" Mike asked.

"Why?"

Mike grinned a little shyly. "I feel sort of funny. All those pulses coming and going and I can't see 'em."

"They haven't bothered you so far."

"I didn't know about 'em, Mac."

"All right, you do the cooking. They can't get down in the galley."

As Mike banged around in the galley, Pete watched the dim sunlight fading out while the darkness of night seemed to seep down through the clouds toward the sea. The wind had shifted more than ninety degrees and was falling so that soon, Pete thought with part of his mind, they ought to shake out those reefs and get along.

Then, almost imperceptibly, it became dark. Pete was startled when Mike turned on the lights in the cabin and the skylights glowed yellow ahead of him. "Mike!" Pete yelled.

Mike came to the companionway.

"Pull the shades on the skylights, will you?"

"What for?"

"So Weber can't see us. It's clearing fast."

"What difference does it make? He can see us with the gizmo anyway."

"Pull 'em," Pete said shortly.

Mike came slowly up the ladder. "Listen, bub," he said slowly, "you're not in the Navy now, see?"

Pete looked steadily in the boy's direction. "Mike, pull the shades on the skylights," he said quietly. "During chow we'll discuss the Navy angle."

"Have it your own way, Mac. But don't start throwing your weight around."

"I'll try not to," Pete said.

The little flare-up worried Pete. Coming on top of the radar, it seemed even worse than it was. Pete hoped that he was no arbitrary martinet who gave orders just to see people jump; but he knew from bitter experience what it was like to be in a sloppy ship where there was no discipline.

Mike came on deck with two plates of food and, in silence, put them down and went below for the coffee. When he came back, he and Pete both ate in silence for a long time; each waiting for the other to begin it.

At last Pete put down his plate. "Mike," he said.

"Go ahead," Mike said.

"Let's get squared away."

Mike put his plate down. To Pete it looked as though he had slammed it down. "Suits me right down to the ground, Mac," Mike said, his voice belligerent. "As long as you don't start throwing out your chest and pushing me around, we're all squared away."

"Good," Pete said quietly. "But this is a ship, and there can only be one master in a ship. Do you want to be the captain or do you want me to be?"

"Don't hand me any of that old Navy bushwa," Mike said. "This is nothing but an old wooden tub, and it doesn't need a captain."

"It's going to have one," Pete said. "We're not

Sunday-sailing around the harbor. We're up against a vicious, smart joe who wouldn't hesitate to kill us both any longer than he hesitated to slap you in the puss with a pistol. We're starting a dangerous journey, Mike, where a split second may decide whether somebody gets hurt or not. That means that one of us has got to obey the other one."

"I don't take orders from nobody," Mike said surlily.

Pete clamped his jaw for a moment and then said, his voice still controlled and quiet, "All right. Then do you think you're the man to give the orders aboard this ship?"

Pete saw Mike's head turn toward him. "Do you mean you'd let me be captain around here?"

"One of us has got to be captain. No matter what *you* think she is, this is still a ship."

Mike put sugar in a coffee cup and then, holding his thumb down in the cup to measure with, he slowly poured coffee in the darkness. Pete watched the blur of his hand as he stirred the sugar slowly, the spoon clanking on the metal rim of the cup.

"Okay," he said at last, "have it your way, 'Captain.'"

His voice was unpleasant, sneering. Pete shook his head. "I don't want it that way, Mike," he said.

Mike stood up, the cup in his hand. "Don't get

me to crying, bub," he said. Before Pete could answer, he went down the ladder and Pete heard the cabin door shut.

Pete slowly poured out a cup of coffee and sat on the wheelbox drinking it. Now, he thought, I've got two problems on my hands. And I can't handle either one of them. Behind me is the radar. Below is Mike.

Two problems? Pete asked himself. No. Three. There's Johnny lying in a narrow white bed, and he can wiggle his right thumb.

For a long time Pete sat there feeling as though he were at the bottom of one of those "pile-ons" they used to play in school. The pile, pressing down on him, grew heavier and heavier. Weber, and Mike, and Johnny. The radar, the reform school, the hospital. The *Santa Ybel*, a .45 automatic, a cathode-ray tube. Johnny and Mike and Weber.

Pete at last shook his head as though to clear his brain. One thing at a time, he thought. Let's tackle one thing first. Which one? He couldn't do a thing about Johnny. Mike? He could do nothing more there. It was up to the kid now. The radar?

Pete looked up at the sails of his ship, gray and ghostly in the dark. Invisible pulses of radio energy were striking them, striking the masts, the hull, the cabin structure. And bouncing back like tattletales to the black sloop. He couldn't stop the evil, invisible things.

And slowly, as his mind drifted, Pete began to remember one night in the Pacific. On Eniwetok Island he had gone ashore and found an old friend of his, Lieutenant "Fish" Fishburne, who was in charge of radar.

Down in Fishburne's Quonset hut the light was dim and eerie and the place was filled with the hum of motors. Across from Fish's desk there was a six-foot transparent disk standing on edge and lit by an indirect glow. In the center of the disk there was a tiny miniature of Eniwetok atoll, from which radiated lines to the outer edge of the disk. A man, stripped to the waist, was sitting behind the disk playing with pieces of colored chalk.

Pete and Fish had been chatting in whispers for nearly an hour when suddenly a quiet voice said, "Bogy, sir."

Fish moved fast. Bending over the big radar scope, he looked at the faint, dim green blotch on the outer rim. For a moment he watched it as the green search line went slowly around and around the cathode tube. Then he picked up a telephone.

"Captain Cruise? Argus. Enemy planes at 350, distance eighty-six miles," Fish reported.

Dimly through the earth above the Quonset Pete heard the air-raid sirens wailing over the island. Fish moved to a high stool in front of the radar scope and everyone in the hut stopped talking.

The man behind the plastic disk adjusted his headphones and picked up a piece of red chalk. On the outer rim of the disk he began to write rapidly, the red numerals glowing. He wrote backward so that those in front of the disk could read it.

Pete was a little startled when Fish said calmly, "Looks like a couple of dozen. Boring straight in."

The green blotch was moving slowly in toward the center of the dimly lit face of the scope. Pete could feel that even Fishburne was growing tense.

Then an operator said, "Isn't that phantom, sir?"

Fish leaned over the scope for a few seconds. "Right you are, Cassidy. Good work!"

"What is it?" Pete whispered.

"It's a trick they try to play on us. See the big green blotch? That's phantom. Here, actually, are the planes," Fish said, pointing to a dimmer green spot in the center of the big blotch of green. "They drop streamers of aluminum foil out of the planes and it registers on the scope as a big cloud. Then they try to sneak in by getting in front of it while we are distracted by the phantom. The stuff is held up by parachutes or paper balloons. But it doesn't work; that is, if you got a heads-up operator like Cassidy. Cassidy can work the planes right through a cloud of phantom."

A voice from a loudspeaker said quietly, "All batteries on target."

And then Pete heard and felt the AA start. There was the sound, so familiar to him, the "pom, pom, pom," but under the ground it sounded soft and far away.

In a little while the sentry stuck his head in and said, "They've hit three of 'em, Mr. Fishburne."

Then there was silence, except for the steady pom, pom, pom of the guns, and Fish studied the scope.

"They'll be dropping us some little presents in a minute. See, they're right over the island."

Pete watched the now bright green blotch moving in fast toward the little picture of the atoll on the disk, the man behind it writing backwards as fast as he could.

"They got two more!" the sentry said, and went out again.

"Those bombs are probably on the way down now," Fish said. "Ever hear 'em, Pete? Close up? Sound like a dog lapping mush out of a bowl."

"I've heard 'em," Pete said.

Then there was the solid ca-rump, ca-rump, ca-rump of the bombs.

"Blast!" Fish said. "They sound like they're

right on top of my tent. Hope they don't bust my shaving mirror."

The sentry stuck his head in. "The Marines are murderin' 'em!" he said, his voice excited. "They're falling all over the place."

Pete went out through the blackout screen and stood pressed against the earth beside the sentry. Plumes of ugly yellow fire were tumbling from the sky while hard bright bursts of AA lit up everything. . . .

Phantom, Pete thought, sitting on the wheel-box of the *Indra* and steering her west as the storm died. Phantom.

And then Pete remembered one morning in a ship chandler's in Miami. He wanted some cheap canvas to make an awning for the cockpit so that the man operating the air pump wouldn't bake in the sun.

The clerk had said, "Canvas? Mister, that's scarcer than nylon. But if you just want to make an awning I've got something here that ought to do pretty well temporarily." He pointed to some three-foot cylinders wrapped in brown paper. "Aluminum foil. We bought a lot of it surplus. Don't know what the Army used it for, but if you put it on a framework, it ought to make a good awning. And it's cheap."

And in the after lazaret there was now on the *Indra* a roll of aluminum foil.

Phantom.

Pete hesitated a moment and then rang the buzzer for Mike. The boy came up the ladder slowly and stood in silence in the cockpit.

"Mike, will you please take the wheel for a little while?" Pete asked, trying to keep his voice quiet and completely impersonal.

Mike stood for a moment silently and then he said, "Sure." Then there was a long pause and he added in a low voice, "Skipper."

Pete grinned in the darkness. Suddenly he felt happier than he had for a long time. But he didn't want to push Mike and so he said, "I think I've got a way to stop that radar, Mike."

"Yeah? How?"

"Phantom," Pete said.

"Phantom? What's that, something to haunt a house?"

"Something to haunt a radar," Pete said.

Dinghy Adrift

It was now night, and the only light showing from the *Indra* since Mike had pulled the curtains across the skylights in the cabin was the dim yellow glow from the compass binnacle. This could hardly be seen outside the cockpit. As Mike took over the wheel,

Pete went forward along the pitching deck and unlashed the long spinnaker boom. Balancing it somewhat like a tightrope walker, he brought it aft and put it down athwartships of the cockpit, the boom sticking out past the ship at both ends.

"Our only chance, Mike," Pete said as he tied the boom so it wouldn't slide overboard, "is to produce on Weber's radar screen another 'pip.' Then we hide behind it and—silently steal away. During the war the Japs tried it, and we called it 'phantom.' And we called the stuff we used 'window.' I don't know what the British called theirs."

"Pips. Phantoms," Mike said. "Sounds like pig Latin to me."

Pete laughed as he went below to get a coil of light rope. Topside again, he rigged shrouds to one end of the boom and moved it out of the way. Then he went forward, unlashed the small dinghy, and brought it back into the cockpit. As he put it down, he patted the smooth plywood bow with his hand. "If this doesn't work we're out one darn good little boat," Pete said.

With Mike helping him, the wheel in beckets, Pete stepped the long boom down through the forward thwart of the dinghy and secured it there with the shrouds he had made. In the darkness the dinghy looked a little like one of the tiny racing-class boats with a very tall mast.

"I don't think she'll carry that much mast," Mike said, looking at it dubiously.

"I don't either." Pete went forward and robbed the fourteen-foot tender of a small anchor. With the rope he made a bridle so that the anchor would hang down in the water several feet below the dinghy and directly under the mast. "That ought to lower her center of gravity enough."

"Won't it slow her down?"

"The slower the better, Mike. We're going to try to sneak out from under that pip, so we don't want it following us."

"Okay, Einstein," Mike said. "I still don't get it."

"You will." Pete then began putting lengths of rope down from the shrouds to the bottom of the dinghy. Since the mast was to carry no sail, Pete ran a rope from the top of the mast to the stern, then he laced lengths of rope between this and the dinghy seats, too. When he at last finished, Mike inspected the work in the darkness and said, "Looks like a bird cage to me."

"It's going to look worse," Pete said as he went below.

He brought up the roll of aluminum foil and some shears. Unrolling it the length of the cockpit, Pete sat down and began cutting out long, thin strips.

"Paper dolls?" Mike asked from the wheel.

Pete flipped his lower lip with two fingers and made a noise like "jibberty, jibberty, jibberty."

"Slow down at the next corner and I'll get off," Mike said.

Pete chuckled. "Now," he said when he had a pile of the strips, "get her steadied down so she'll sail no hands."

"When I'm on the wheel, Mac, I keep my ship trimmed up," Mike said indignantly.

"I'd forgotten," Pete said. He went over then, started the engine, and when it was running smoothly at slow throttle, he eased it into gear.

Pete then began unlaying the ropes he had tied to the dinghy and slipping the aluminum strips in between the lays. As soon as he turned loose, the new rope laid up again, clamping the strips tightly. When strips were in all the ropes as high as the cockpit coaming, Pete stopped.

"Now come the crucial minutes," he said. "As I build up the area of these strips, you've got to reduce the area of the sail."

"Tell me something, Mac," Mike said. "Do you know what you're doing?"

"I wish I knew," Pete said. "All I know is that little millionth-of-a-second radio pulses are hitting us like a man shooting an endless stream of invisible bird shot at us. When they hit, they bounce right back to Weber and produce a flickering green line.

"Now Weber's been looking at that line for a long time. He knows how bright and how big it is. If we throw all this tinfoil in front of those radio pulses without, at the same time, reducing the area they can hit, that line is going to get brighter and bigger and Weber is going to sit up straight and say, 'Ah, dirty work at the crossroads.' "

"The boy's a genius," Mike said as he got up and stood by the main halyard.

Pete rapidly inserted the strips into the rest of the ropes as Mike slowly, and at the word, lowered the mainsail. He then lowered the foresail, and when Pete put in the last strip, Mike let the jib down with a run.

As Mike took sail off her slowly, Pete kept touching the throttle so that there was no change in the *Indra's* speed. He had also kept an eye on the compass and had shifted the beckets to keep the *Indra* on a straight course.

When Mike jumped down into the cockpit again, Pete put the pelorus on top of the compass and tied a penlight flashlight in the stern of the dinghy. At last he stood up and looked aft into the inky darkness.

"Well, here goes all or nothing," Pete said. "Let's get her over the side."

The little dinghy with the spinnaker boom sticking up straight and tall out of her was unwieldly, and they had a hard time getting it down into the rough water. For a little while, to see how she was going to float, they kept the painter secured and towed the dinghy along, the aluminum strips fluttering metallically in the wind and faintly glistening even in the darkness.

"That certainly does look like one big piece of foolishness," Mike declared.

"If you're right, we're sunk," Pete said. "Well, I think she'll take it without capsizing." Lying down and reaching, he turned the penlight on. "Let her go," he said.

Mike pulled the painter through the ringbolt and the dinghy, completely free, swung slowly around until her bow was into the wind. The penlight made a tiny bright spot which appeared and disappeared as the waves ran before the wind.

Pete went back to the pelorus on the compass. "There's his pip," he said. "And all we've got to do is to keep the dinghy exactly between us and him so that the pip we make won't appear through the stronger pip made by that foil. Got a pencil?"

Mike got a notebook and pencil out of the chart case. "Shoot," he said.

Pete sighted through the pelorus at the penlight. The pelorus was, in principle, exactly like the iron sights of a rifle. By lining up two slits, one on each side of the compass, so that you could see an object, you could read the bearing of the object from the ship by looking into mirrors which reflected the compass card.

"Forty-six," Pete said.

"Forty-six," Mike repeated, writing it down.

"Fifty-one—she's yawing all over the ocean."

"Fifty-one," Mike said.

"Forty-five."

"Forty-five."

"Forty-two."

"Forty-two."

"Forty-six."

"Forty-six."

"Forty-eight. She's getting dim, Mike."

"Forty-eight."

"Fifty-two."

"Fifty-two."

"Fifty. If we hold 225, I think it'll be good enough."

"Fifty."

Pete went on taking readings until, at last, he could no longer see the spark of the penlight. Quickly he added up the readings Mike had entered, divided them by the number of readings taken, and added 180 degrees to the result. "Put her right on 223 and hold her, Mike. Don't let her move an inch if you can help it." Pete then shoved the throttle all the way forward and came back to the wheel. Taking it over from Mike, he did not lift his eyes from the compass card as he steered, holding the lubber's line steady as a rock on 223.

After a few minutes Mike said in a low voice, "What do you think, Skipper?"

Pete didn't move his eyes. "I don't think anything, but here's what I hope. First, that the new pip we made was big enough to cover up the pip the *Indra* was making—but not so big that it would make him suspicious. Second, that, when we let the dinghy go adrift, the speed was quickly reduced. Weber would not notice it at once and would keep coming at his same speed. This would make the pip of the dinghy grow brighter and bigger. Third, when Weber noticed that the pip was growing, he slowed down to keep from over-running us. Fourth, he wondered what we were up to but, as soon as the dinghy started yawing around, Weber relaxed, deciding that we had heaved the *Indra* to. Last—he's heaved to, also, watching the pip of the dinghy."

"But if it wanders all over the place, why can't he see the one we make?"

"I'm afraid of that," Pete said. "But there's hope. You see, the pip moving up and down the scale the way the dinghy's is leaves a sort of luminous trail behind it. I'm hoping that that trail will blot out the pip we make."

"Okay," Mike said. "I don't understand it. So all I want to know is—did we or didn't we?"

"Brother," Pete said in a whisper, "so do I."

"So when do we find out?"

"We find out, Mike, when the sun shines again, when there's not a cloud in the sky and you, astride the crosstree with the glasses, either—see a black sloop or don't see a black sloop."

"You mean we've got to go on like this until tomorrow—or maybe even the next day?"

Pete nodded.

"Holy cow!" Mike said. "I'll be a nervous wreck."

"It isn't so bad," Pete said. "I've been a nervous wreck ever since Weber poked his black sloop out of those clouds this afternoon."

"Say, Mac," Mike said suddenly. "How far can that gimmick see, anyway? Suppose this storm clears up tonight—it's dying fast now—and the sun shines first thing in the morning. And right in front of Weber is that dinghy with all the Christmas tree decorations on it. What's to keep him from turning a knob or something and seeing us again?"

As Pete started to answer, the ship's clock in the companionway tinkled eight bells.

"It's midnight now," Pete said. "Sunrise in the morning is about five thirty-two. That gives us five hours of darkness, Mike. In that time, with the wind aft, we can make better than thirty miles. Without the sails up at thirty miles I don't think the little set Weber's got can see us. His antenna is down on his mast just above the jib stay, which is pretty low for surface search, and we don't stick out of the water more than ten feet, except for the masts. I think he'd bust a cathode trying to see us that far."

"Suppose the engine conks out?" Mike suggested.

"I've got plenty of trouble without you thinking up any more," Pete said. "But you might drop down into the engine room and see if she's still ticking. Feel the intake water line on the starboard side—if it isn't fairly cool, holler. Can you short a plug?"

"That business with the screw driver?"

"Yep. Be sure the blade of the screw driver is on the engine before the shank touches the plug lead."

"I'll do it but it always bites me," Mike said.

"And check the gas and oil."

Mike got up. "If the engine comes up through the deck with me on top of it, you'll know I did something wrong," he said.

Soon Pete heard the engine skipping. He counted the times and relaxed when it skipped four times. Soon Mike came topside again. "Say, that works all right. Didn't bite me a single time."

"Everything all right?"

"Running like a nose," Mike said. "Couldn't be better. Cool, too."

"Good. Why don't you turn in?"

"Are you nuts? I want to be here when Weber draws up alongside with our dinghy and says, 'Hey, you dropped something.' "

"That's what I like about you," Pete said. "You

always look on the bright side of things. Go below and catch some sack time. We've got a long way to go yet and all of it running like a rabbit."

"I couldn't sleep," Mike declared. "I'd get to dreaming about those radio things flying back and forth and I'd have nightmares."

"Try it anyway," Pete insisted.

"All right. But I'll be screamin' in five minutes."

"Scream away. I'm used to it."

Pete felt lonely after Mike left. The night was pitch-black, the storm clouds blanking out the stars and the moon. The dying storm no longer tormented the sea, and it was now as black as the night except for the weird trail of faint green phosphorus which faded away behind the *Indra* and foamed around her long, sleek hull so that she seemed to be sailing in a trough of wavering green water.

Pete listened for Mike's nightmares, but no wild screams came up the companion ladder. The motor, its underwater exhaust throbbing, hummed steadily and its sound was so smooth, so constant, that after a while Pete no longer heard it. He sat in loneliness, his eyes always on the compass card, steering down the invisible line made by 223 degrees.

Once he took his left hand off the wheel spoke and looked at it under the dim yellow light from the binnacle. Then he stretched his arm out slowly. It would not go out straight. Then, in the darkness, he tried to touch his shoulder with his fingers but he could not. And he tried to touch his shoulder blades, and he could not. He thought of the Navy Cross thrown carelessly into a drawer in Mr. Williams's apartment. And the Purple Heart—a pretty purple-and-gold medal—beside the Navy Cross.

But as bitterness started to rise in him Pete remembered Ward Twenty at Oak Knoll. That was where the men with no hands, no legs, were. They were the real Purple Heart people. Pete put his left hand back on the wheel spoke.

Slowly the storm died but the clouds of storm, as though reluctant, as though they had not finished their brutal teasing of the sea, did not disappear from the sky for a long time. The night ebbed, the seas calmed, the wind settled in a new and gentle quarter.

And for the first time since he had left Miami —a time which seemed to Pete almost as remote as the time of war—the sun came up. Bright and clean and innocent, it lifted itself from the calm sea. Waves sparkled, the deep blue was back. Flying fish skittered ahead of the ship.

There were three clouds in the sky. One far to the south was grayish and low—the end of the storm. One to the west was a little white puffball which seemed not to know what it was doing

up there. And one to the north was just a thin line of haze.

Pete pressed the buzzer. Almost immediately Mike appeared in a pair of his new skivvy pants. "'Oh, what a beautiful mah'nin',' " he sang. "Where's old Pickle Puss?"

"Get the glasses," Pete said.

Before Mike opened the compartment, he

looked slowly all around the empty horizon. "Can't see him from here," he said.

"Aloft is where it counts," Pete said.

Mike got the glasses and started climbing hand over hand up the main halyard. Halfway up to the crosstrees, he yelled down, "Pete, suppose I see him?"

Pete felt cold in his stomach, almost sick. "Just say so, I guess, Mike."

"Okay." Mike's voice sounded cheerful.

Pete glanced up once as Mike reached the crosstrees and slung a leg over one of them. Then, just looking straight ahead, Pete waited. Time seemed to flow like warm asphalt. The clock in the companionway tinkled sweetly four times.

Pete wanted to look up at the tiny figure high in the air swaying with the mast slowly from side to side, but he did not. He wanted to call out, "What's the word?" as he knew that Mike was moving the glasses inch by inch, covering all the sparkling sea enclosed by the circle of the horizon, but he did not.

Minutes—to Pete, hours—went by, and Mike made no sound. At last Pete could stand it no longer, and he looked aloft.

Mike wasn't there.

Pete froze for an instant, and then Mike jumped calmly down into the cockpit, put the binoculars in the case, and put it back into the compartment. To Pete he seemed to do everything as slowly as he could.

"Empty as a plate," Mike said. "Not a ship in sight."

Then, standing in front of Pete, he stuck out his hand. "You did it . . . Cap'n," Mike said. "Now, how about we eat a little snack?"

Book Three

SECRET SEA

Hideaway

The *Indra* was eleven days out of Miami and far into the Gulf. After the storm died, the weather was perfect, with a Beaufort 4 wind which never went forward of the beam. Two or three times each day, and always at sunrise, either Mike or Pete climbed the sail hoops to the crosstrees and scanned the sea, but the black sloop never appeared again. Pete continued to worry, for he knew that the height of the crosstrees and the height of the mast of the sloop did not give a total visibility equal to the maximum range of the radar, but as the days went by he worried less. They had passed many ships and sailboats, and for one entire night they had followed close in the wake of a slow freighter and for a day they had changed course a good deal to sail side by side with a schooner loaded with lumber en route to Jamaica. As the eleventh day ended with a beautiful sunset, Pete became convinced that they had lost Weber. He reasoned that, even if Weber had picked them up again on the radar after finding the dinghy, he would not have been able to identify the *Indra*.

"He's probably chased every yacht and slow freight in the Gulf," Pete said.

"How do you know he's not just over the horizon?" Mike asked.

"They haven't got radar to the point where it can talk yet," Pete said. "Since we gave Weber a very fine dinghy, he must have had a dozen pips on the scope. To find out if we were making them, he would have to come within visible range,

Mike. He's got a Marconi-rigged boat—getting a man up on the mast is quite a performance. I think, rather than go to all the trouble of lowering the sail and rigging a bosun's chair, Weber would close up on any pip he saw until he could identify it from the deck. After all, Mike, he knows that as soon as he spots us again he's got us licked."

"He may know it," Mike said, his voice belligerent, "but we don't know it. We've already turned his damper down twice. Next time we'll fix his clock so it really won't run."

"I'd rather not have a next time," Pete said, going over and rigging the radio compass loop.

Mike, on the wheel, looked up at the sails glimmering in the starlit darkness. "He hit me with a pistol," Mike said slowly. "I haven't forgotten that."

Pete listened to the signals from two shore stations and drew a thin-lined X on the chart. Then he walked a pair of dividers southward. He turned off the compass, stowed the loop, and shoved the chart back in the case. "Mike, me boy, our ETA is five bells in the morning watch."

"Listen, Skipper," Mike said with mock plaintiveness, "I'm just a poor civilian. I didn't go out and win no war with one hand tied behind my back."

"I mean that at six-thirty in the morning two

173

islands should appear. One of them is almost barren—just a rock-and-sand job—and the other is a little number with bending palms, et cetera. Keep an eye out for 'em."

"Is that where the *Santa Ybel* is?"

"Close by."

"So by tomorrow night we'll have the old *Indra* loaded with gold," Mike said jubilantly.

"Hold hard, sailor," Pete said. "By tomorrow night you'll have so many blisters on your hands you'll think they're hamburgers. And I hope there aren't any mosquitoes on that island."

"Blisters? What do you mean, blisters?"

"You know, little round things. Juicy. Because we're taking the masts out."

"Oh, for the love of my uncle Ned—what for?"

"Radar," Pete said. "We're going to make the smallest possible area for that thing to see. There's a lot of metal high up on those masts. They're coming out."

"Aw, Pete, for heaven's sake!" Mike grumbled. "You're an old maid. Why don't we just scoop up that gold and get out of here? You mess around with masts and things, and it just gives Weber that much more time to find us."

"Mike, that stuff can't just be 'scooped' up. It's going to take us days, maybe weeks, maybe months to get it," Pete said slowly. "We've got to find the ship first. She's only something over two hundred feet long. Two hundred feet in a million miles isn't very much."

"I thought you knew where she was. Up there in that brain of yours. That's what you said," Mike accused him.

"I know where the *Santa Ybel* is, all right," Pete said patiently. "What I don't know is where we are."

"What about that radio thing you're always fooling with? Doesn't that tell you where you are?"

Pete nodded. "But I've already plotted the possible positions we can get from the stations we can hear down here. The nearest fix puts us close to the *Santa Ybel* . . . but we've still got to find her. She's been there for four hundred years, Mike. Ever see a barnacle?"

"On my uncle's neck," Mike said.

"In four hundred years the barnacles and coral will be thick on her. Ten . . . twenty . . . thirty feet maybe. We've got to cut or blast through that. Then maybe we've got to cut a hole in her if I can't get down through the hatches. And finally, when we do find the gold, we've got to get it out and up, which, if that one piece is as big as the wheel of an oxcart, will be quite an operation all by itself."

"H'mmm," Mike said. "Hadn't thought of all that."

"So in the morning we do a little tooth pulling and a little painting," Pete said.

Pete's ETA was right on the nose. As the sun
came up, the two islands were dead ahead of
them. As Pete circled the barren one, Mike stood
beside the wheel looking out over the sparkling
sea.

"Where is she, Captain?" Mike asked in a low voice.

"Out there," Pete pointed.

"Looks mighty empty."

"Let's worry about that later." Pete turned the *Indra* and sailed for the other island, which looked green and shining in the early morning light.

As they sailed slowly up toward it, the foresail down and only the number two jib and main on her, there appeared to be no harbor at all, just a steep green bank plunging into the sea. But as they came closer, they saw that a narrow reef circled out from the island like the blade of a scimitar and enclosed a beautiful little bay. Bright green mangroves grew on the reef, so that the bay was hard to see even when close up on the island.

"If there's a passage through that reef and there's water enough behind it we've got just what the doctor ordered," Pete said. "How about getting the lead line and seeing what we've got for bottom, Mike?"

"How much do we draw?" Mike asked, getting the lead line out of the lazaret.

"Eight feet."

"How much do you want under her?"

"Not much. We've got a lot of solid lead fin down there."

Pete turned the *Indra* and she ghosted along

the reef. The water, in the lee of the island, was glass smooth and as clear as crystal. Mike, standing in the bow, could see fish, lobsters, crabs, and mollusks moving around on the bottom thirty feet down.

Near the northern end of the reef there was a narrow slit. Mike shaded his eyes and studied it and then called back to Pete, "She's mighty narrow, Skipper, but she looks deep."

"We'll try it. Take the jib off, will you?"

Pete put the *Indra* into the wind, swung the main boom over the gallows frame, and dropped her down. Then he took the sails off and started the engine.

Going ahead at dead slow, Pete standing on the wheelbox, Mike in the bow with the lead, the *Indra* moved toward the slit in the reef.

"No bottom at seven," Mike yelled as he checked the run of the line and began retrieving it. On the next heave he got bottom and called out, "By the deep six," as the seven-fathom red rag stopped in his hand.

The channel through the reef had a dog-leg curve in it and apparently smack in the middle was a huge castle of brain coral.

"Stop her," Mike called. Then he aimed the lead at the coral and heaved. The lead splashed and sank in a trail of bubbles and Mike let them clear until he could see the lead lying gray on the white coral head. "Now come ahead dead slow," he called. "There's a coral head we either get over or we don't."

The *Indra* came ahead so slowly that she seemed not to be moving at all. Mike kept the lead line taut as the bow moved inch by inch over the coral head. At last when the lead line was straight up and down, Mike sang out, "And a half, one. Come ahead."

The *Indra* moved ahead, the deep fin keel clearing the coral head by less than a foot. Pete turned her down the dog-leg, and she slid smoothly into the bay.

Mike kept singing out the soundings, but the bay had an almost uniform depth of ten feet almost to the sandy beach.

"Stand by the anchor," Pete called. "Let her go."

Mike watched the QED anchor fall in front of the bubbles, then turn lazily over as Pete reversed the engine. The flukes dug into the white sand, the chain came taut.

Pete cut the engine, and suddenly everything seemed lonely and silent. Mike came aft and stood in the cockpit looking in silence at the little island, with the coconut palms ringing the beach all curving in the same direction.

"First thing—we go ashore and see if anyone is around," Pete said.

"Let's swim," Mike said. "That water looks good, doesn't it?"

"It really does," Pete said. He got up on the companion cover and looked around. "Don't jump in right now," he said quietly as Mike put a leg over the life line.

"Why not?"

"See that little ripple?"

Mike looked where he was pointing and jerked

180

his leg back over the life line. "Holy mackerel!"

A shark curved slowly in toward the *Indra* and coasted down the starboard side. Mike peered down at it goggle-eyed as it turned a little on one side and looked up at him with its cold, vicious little eye.

"Guess we'll have to use the boat," Mike said. "And I wanted to go swimming."

"We'll swim," Pete said. "Just wait a minute."

Pete came up from the cabin with a little yellow packet the size of a cake of soap but wrapped in waterproof plastic. "Where'd he go?" he asked.

Mike pointed to the fin slicing calmly along twenty feet away.

Pete removed the wrapping and broke off a piece of the stuff that looked like soap. He threw it at the shark, and the fish circled away from it and then came back to investigate it as it floated on the water.

From the floating stuff a solid circle of black dye began to form in the water, spreading farther and farther. The shark, swimming lazily, suddenly turned, the fin sizzling through the water, and went toward the beach. As though suddenly blind, he almost grounded on the sand before he turned and whipped across the lagoon. The water boiled down the narrow channel as the shark escaped into the open ocean.

Mike stooped down slowly and picked up the

yellow wrapping. " 'U.S.N.,' " he read on it. " 'Shark Repellent.' "

"Shark chaser," Pete said. "Works."

"Drove that one crazy all right. What's it made out of?"

"You'd be surprised," Pete said. "It's made out of what comes out of dead sharks—copper acetate. The Navy never would have discovered a good chaser if it hadn't been for an old Florida shark fisherman. He just happened to mention that if he left a dead shark on his hooks other sharks wouldn't come near it after it had been dead for a day or so. That put the Navy on the track, and for a long time the Navy played around with dead sharks until they found what was in the corpses which drove away live sharks. Must have been a little smelly."

"Does it always work?" Mike asked.

"I guess that's a little like a parachute. If it doesn't work, you can always take it back and get a new one—if you happen to be alive."

Mike looked around the lagoon. "No mo' sharks." With a run he cleared the life line, sailed out, and landed in the water flat on his belly. Pete heard him grunt when he hit.

"Just like a swan," Pete said as Mike came up still gasping for breath.

"Don't get smart," Mike said angrily. "You try it."

Pete cleared the life line too. But then he couldn't find the water. It was so crystal-clear that he couldn't see the surface at all—just the white sand bottom. He was thinking that he had another foot or so to fall when he hit flat on his face, his eyes wide open. It knocked him dizzy for a minute, and when he looked around, Mike was treading water and laughing. "Just like a log," Mike said.

They swam ashore together, and on the beach Pete said, "You go around that way, I'll go this. Look out for old fires, footprints, shacks, and stuff."

In fifteen minutes Pete looked up to see Mike coming toward him. "Not a sign of anything but pelicans," Mike said. "I don't believe a human being has ever been on this island."

"I haven't seen anything either. But let's take one trip over the top."

They came out on the beach without having seen any trace of people. The *Indra* lay white and calm on the clear water, wind rattled softly in the coconut palms.

"Let's get to work," Pete said, wading out into the water. "You stay ashore and I'll heave you a line. We'll warp the *Indra* in as close as we can, careen her, and rig some sort of tackle to pull out the masts.

It was hard, hot work, and by nightfall Pete

and Mike both had blisters on their hands from the long hauling on the ropes. But both masts were out of the *Indra* and concealed up among the trees, the sails stowed below.

"Looks sort of naked," Mike said, looking out at the ship.

"Looks like a pooch somebody just threw a bucket of cold water on. I feel sort of sorry for her. But she wouldn't show on a radar now unless it was set up on the reef. Not with the island behind her that way."

"So tomorrow we go get some gold, huh?"

Pete shook his head. "Tomorrow we paint. You can use either green paint, gray paint, brown paint, or black paint, or all four. But by tomorrow night we want the *Indra* to be the biggest mess of paint you ever saw. We want to paint lines and curves and patches and blobs."

"She looks all right white," Mike said.

"Just like a sore thumb," Pete said. "Tomorrow we camouflage her."

"Skipper, if it wasn't for the chow, I'd mutiny," Mike said. "Here we are with gold all over the bottom of the ocean and what do we do? Do we go get some of it? No. We paint. We haul wood. We mess around."

Pete laughed. "Go mess around in the galley while I rig a sounding chain. And those last pancakes you cooked could have been used for collision mats."

"Okay, horrible, you cook," Mike said.

"Suits me. You go forward and measure off exactly one hundred and five feet of anchor chain and flemish it down the starboard deck."

Mike turned toward the ladder. "How'd you say you liked your pancakes, Cap'n? Soft and fluffy or thin and soggy?"

"I just like plenty of 'em," Pete said, and went forward to the anchor chain.

Contact

Three days later a strange ship emerged from the
lagoon. The *Indra*, bare of masts and bowsprit, of
boom and gaff and gallows frame, looked unfin-
ished and ashamed. She was like a car without
wheels, an airplane without wings. Close up she
also looked like the mixing vats of a paint factory.

186

"A sailboat's got no business looking like this," Mike said sorrowfully.

"It hurts," Pete admitted. "But she'll give that radar a headache."

"Maybe the radar can't find her but I don't know about all this paint. It seems to me that she'd be easier to spot this way than when she was plain white."

"Doesn't work that way, really," Pete said. "I saw battleships painted this way and you couldn't see 'em until you were right on top of them."

Pete had followed the Navy's camouflage system—breaking all the straight lines, fixing places where shadows would fall so that the shadows wouldn't show, making the painted patches and blobs appear to flow down into the water. All the shades were pale—thin greens and grays and browns.

"We'll find out," Mike said. "When Weber sails right by us in that black sloop, I'll give you six bottle caps."

"It's a deal."

On the high tide the *Indra* slipped out of the channel, and Pete turned her west.

"What do we do now?" Mike asked. "I bet you've got 'steen more things to do before we go after that gold. I'm beginning to believe you don't want to find it."

"Mike, me lad, calm yourself. And go forward.

Let the anchor chain run out until that red rag tied in it is just clear of the hawsehole."

"That sounds more like treasure hunting," Mike said as he went forward. On the end of the anchor chain was a small grapnel and Mike dropped it and watched it foam down as the anchor chain rattled out of the chain locker. The red rag flashed by, and Mike snubbed the chain and then cranked it back in until the rag was at the hawsehole.

Back in the cockpit, Mike asked, "What happens now?"

"When we were testing that gimmick for BuShips, the water to the north of the *Santa Ybel* had a fairly uniform depth of a hundred and ten feet," Pete explained. "The grapnel is down to a hundred and five. We'll get as close to the position as we can with the radio compass and then work a square search until the grapnel hooks something. When she does, we drop a buoy."

Mike looked at him. "You mean we leave a buoy out there with a sign on it, 'Here's the gold, Mr. Weber'?"

Pete grinned and pointed to an old, dried, brown, hard coconut lying in the stern. Mike picked it up. A lag screw with a ring in it had been screwed into the coconut. A snap hook attached to a reel of thin stainless-steel wire was snapped into the ring. On the other end of the wire there was a small folding anchor such as those used for anchoring small sailboats.

Mike laughed. "If I didn't know you so well, Cap'n, I'd think you were a genius."

But Pete had put on the headphones and was plotting his position as the *Indra* moved slowly ahead. Slowly, dot by dot, across the chart a line moved toward a red dot Pete had made. As he listened to the sounds coming from the earphones and slowly revolved the loop of the compass, Pete got tense. His mouth got dry and then his throat, and soon he could hear his heart beating so loud that it almost interfered with the compass signals. Pete licked his dry teeth, but when he made another dot, he noticed that his hand was trembling.

Then Mike said, his voice breaking, "Boy, this is worse than walking around a haunted house. Suppose we miss her, Pete?"

Pete didn't answer. The line was coming closer and closer. Once he looked up, looked forward at the calm, blue, soft water.

Then the line of the *Indra's* course sliced through the red dot. Pete picked up a packet of aviator's dye marker and threw it overboard. Slowly on the blue water a deep green dye began to spread.

"That's where she's supposed to be," Pete said quietly. "Mike, go up and put your hand on the

chain. Maybe she touched but the grapnel didn't catch anything. If you feel a contact, let out a whoop."

Mike ran forward and lay down on his stomach beside the hawsehole. Putting his hand on the up-and-down chain, he looked through the metal hole at the water.

After a while Pete took the headphones off. "Must have missed her," he called to Mike.

Standing on top of the wheelbox so he could see the green splotch of dye, Pete turned the *Indra* around and went back. As the bows of the ship slid into the green stain on the blue water, Pete held his breath.

Mike saw the water turn from blue to green and he gripped the chain hard, feeling for any tremor.

Pete let his breath out slowly as the green showed up astern. Mike relaxed his grip on the chain.

They went back and forth through the green dye until it faded and disappeared. The hanging chain touched nothing.

Pete called Mike aft. "We're getting haphazard and this is too big an ocean," Pete said quietly. "We'll run up another position line and then work out a sector search on definite courses. That way we'll at least know what water we've been through. You steer."

"I hope she's still down there," Mike said.

Pete looked at him but said nothing.

It was well on into the afternoon before they finished the first sector. Both of them were tired, not only from the strain of steering to a hair's breadth on the compass but also from that of waiting for the grapnel to catch and slow them. They ate some lunch out of cans—ate in silence—and then went back to the dogged tracing of the sea. The clock in the companionway tinkled off the bells as the afternoon dragged on. It had been more than an hour since Mike had said, "We've been over this spot a dozen times. I recognize the waves."

Pete couldn't even grin. Ever since two o'clock he had been wondering if the marvelous sounding device on the PC had been as accurate as he had thought it was. As the *Indra* searched mile after square mile of sea, each area overlapping the position the detector had given him, Pete wondered. If the thing was not accurate, he and Mike might just as well go home, for they would never find the *Santa Ybel* by just dragging the ocean.

Time after time Pete checked his position with the radio compass. His head ached from straining to hear the signals, from trying to pick the absolute peak of the beat from each station.

For more than two hours neither he nor Mike had said a word. At the end of each run Pete would turn the ship, come back in on the new course, and settle down, his eyes glued to the compass while Mike lay in silence forward, first one hand, then the other gripping the chain.

The clock tinkled eight times. Pete, listening to the musical sound dying away, debated whether to stop at the end of the next run, drink some coffee, and then go on. After a while they could eat supper, drink some more coffee, and keep on searching until both of them were too tired to keep her on a compass course. It made no difference, Pete decided, whether it was day or night. For four centuries the *Santa Ybel* had been there, and the grapnel on the end of the chain was sightless and without feeling. They might as well search until the wake of the *Indra* stopped flowing out straight as a string, began to waver as fatigue got them.

And then, as though sharp steel fingers had suddenly gripped him and held him motionless, Pete sat for an eternity of time, it seemed to him, without being able to move a muscle as Mike's voice beat into his ears.

"Back her down! *Back her down!* Back her! Back her."

Pete moved at last. He slammed the engine into reverse, shoved the throttle forward. Water churned and foamed up under the *Indra*'s after overhang, and she slowly stopped going forward and began to swim backwards.

"Stop her. Stop her!" Mike yelled.

Pete shoved her into forward gear, knocked the way off her, and then slipped the lever back into neutral. He slowed the racing engine and said, his voice much louder than necessary, "What is it?"

"She's hooked something. Still got it," Mike yelled back.

Pete grabbed the coconut and the reel of wire with the anchor on it and ran forward.

Stooping beside Mike, he felt the anchor chain, felt its resistance. Slowly, with infinite care, as though he were extending the sense of touch all the way down the chain, Pete began to pull upward on it.

He needn't have been so careful. The grapnel was into something solid and when he heaved on it he could feel only coral and barnacles crushing under the hooks of the grapnel.

As the *Indra*, anchored by the grapnel, slowly swung her bow into the gentle wind, Mike said, whispering, "Is it?"

"I don't know," Pete said. He went to the side of the ship and dropped the little anchor so that it plummeted down beside the chain to the grapnel. The steel wire payed out as Pete held the spool with a marlinespike through the center. The bright wire flashed and glittered as it snaked down into the water, and when at last it stopped feeding from the spool, Pete dropped the coconut and watched it bob and float away. It looked like all the rest of the thousands of dried coconuts floating around in the sea.

"If that isn't the *Santa Ybel*," Mike said slowly, "it's going to ruin me, Pete."

"Me too. But we went all over this water in the PC, Mike. We searched the whole bottom around here and there was nothing except what I *hope* is the *Santa Ybel*, and, very near her, a German submarine two planes put the blast on."

"Well," Mike said, "tomorrow tells the tale."

"Tomorrow, my eye," Pete said. "Today. . . . Take these readings, mate."

Mike got a notebook and pencil. Pete, anticipation running wild inside him, forced himself to take slow, careful, accurate readings from the radio compass.

When he finished, he averaged them and wrote the two final bearings in big black letters on the bottom of the page of the notebook. Under them, also big and black, he wrote down the longitude and latitude the detector on the PC had given him.

Then Pete sat down in the cockpit and motioned for Mike to sit beside him. "Here are four sets of numbers, Mike," Pete said quietly. "Look at them—this is the latitude and longitude of the *Santa Ybel*, if she's down there. And these are the bearings from radio compass stations."

"Okay, okay," Mike said impatiently, "so we know where she is. Let's go get some of that old folding stuff."

Pete shook his head. "No, Mike. Memorize these numbers first. Memorize 'em so you can't forget them no matter what happens."

"What for? Holy mackerel, Pete, let's get on with this business. We've been messing around with stuff like this for too long already."

"Memorize 'em, speedy," Pete said. "Because we may not be through with Weber yet."

Mike began repeating the numbers over and over. Finally he said, "Okay, I got 'em. Let's go!"

Pete tore the pages out of the notebook and crumpled them up with the chart. Then he took them below to the galley and burned them. When he came back, lugging the light diving suit and helmet, he said, "Now there's not a piece of writing that Weber can get his hands on that'll do him any good. If he ever finds us the only way he can get those numbers is to beat them out of us. And I don't think he can do it."

"He better not try. You going down now?" Mike asked.

Pete nodded as he began to get into the diving suit.

"You going free?" Mike asked.

Pete grinned as Mike lowered the helmet carefully down over his head. When the faceplate screwed around to the front, Pete shook his head, making a "no" with his lips. Mike got the life line with the telephone connection inside it and attached it to the helmet. As soon as he put the earphones on, Pete turned his throat mike on and said, "Cinch up the chest weights. They feel loose."

Mike obeyed and then Pete said quietly, "Okay, hoist away."

On the stern of the *Indra* a low stout hoist and short boom were rigged where the gallows frame had been. Mike attached the lift to the bridle around Pete and hoisted him up, swung him out over the stern, and lowered him slowly down into the water.

For a few moments Pete lay on his back, bobbing around in the water as he kept the air exhaust valve closed. During the long watches after the storm Pete and Mike had spent hours rehearsing and making dummy runs on the diving equipment. Mike had almost memorized the decompression time for length of time under at a hundred and ten feet. Pete was sure that Mike realized how important it was to watch the clock, the valves, the lines—everything. Pete's life depended on it.

But now, as he actually lay in the water, ready to go down, he waited a moment longer, looking up through the glass faceplate at the boy standing beside the rail, the life line lying in his hands.

He was only a kid, Pete thought. A kid Johnny's age. There wasn't much for him to do when Pete was down. Especially in the self-contained outfit. Nothing to do but watch the hands of a clock go around. And to Pete those clock hands meant either a safe ascent or the agony of the bends.

Pete looked up at Mike once more. "Okay," he said into the throat mike, "I'm going down. Start the stop watch as soon as I go under."

"Got it." Mike's voice came roaring into the helmet.

"Not so loud, the phone works well," Pete said as he turned the exhaust valve.

He went down fast, plummeting straight down, the leads on his feet pulling him. The light faded slowly foot by foot, but Mike's voice seemed close and familiar as he read off the distances.

At eighty feet Pete slowed his rate of descent until by ninety feet he was going down at about a foot a second. Peering through the faceplate, he could see nothing but a dark, empty plain rising as he settled to the bottom of the ocean. It was like the western deserts after the sun had gone down and the dark of night was crowding in upon them.

Pete's heavy feet crunched into the hard sand bottom and he adjusted the exhaust valve so that he could walk easily.

"On bottom," he said.

"What's down there?"

"Looks empty. But there isn't much light."

"You mean she's not there?" Mike's voice asked.

"Don't see her," Pete said.

He turned slowly, swinging one heavy foot wide around and putting it down firmly and then swinging the other one. Air from the oxygen bottle hissed steadily into the top of the helmet and felt cool against the back of his neck. The bubbles of air going into the caustic soda regenerator made a frying sound. And there was coming from the sea a faint crackling, tingling noise which never stopped.

Pete swung another foot around. Ahead of him, looking far away, was a shape: a wall, a block of coral and barnacles. It had no resemblance to a ship—it was just a gray block rising from the white sand of the sea's floor.

"There's something here. I don't know whether it's her or not. Pretty well encrusted," Pete said.

Mike didn't answer but since Pete could hear him breathing into an open phone he didn't worry.

Walking as though in a dream of slow motion, Pete approached the wall which went up beyond the edge of the faceplate. As he came closer, he

He lifted it up in front of the glass.

began to stumble into chunks and piles of broken coral and barnacles scattered across the sand. "Looks like there's been an explosion down here . . . recently," Pete said.

"Does that mean—somebody's been here?" Mike asked.

Then Pete remembered. "Don't think so," he said. "We sank a German sub here in '43. That's probably what scattered this stuff around—or maybe it's just a rocky formation."

But he was close to it then and, through the growing gloom, he saw the rough outlines of a ship's ribs and carlings. They formed a broken skeleton rising from the rubbish which had been blown from the hull of the *Santa Ybel* by the explosion of the depth charges which had killed the sub.

Pete's foot hit something which tinkled, and he bent down, groping with his hands until he found it, and lifted it up in front of the glass. It was a deadeye.

"I'm coming up," Pete said. "How long?"

"Five and a half minutes," Mike said.

"All right, hoist away. Bring me up at thirty feet a minute. Stop me at ten feet and leave me there three and a half minutes."

"Listen, bright boy," Mike said. "I can read."

Pete chuckled. Holding the deadeye in his hand, he relaxed as Mike hoisted him up toward the glow he could see above him. Halfway up he felt an itching between his shoulder blades and started to tell Mike to send him down again, but the itching stopped and nothing else happened, so he kept quiet.

At ten feet Mike stopped him.

"Let's don't play strong and silent, Mac." Mike's voice rang around the helmet. "What'd you see down there?"

"The skeleton of a wooden ship, Mike. And she was under sail because I've got one of her shroud deadeyes."

"What do you think?" Mike asked.

"I think I've been floating around here long enough," Pete said, turning on his back and looking over at the hull of the *Indra* floating dark and long against the glowing water.

"Listen, fathead!" Mike said, his voice ringing in Pete's ears. "I'll cut you loose and leave you down there forever. Talk or, so help me, I'll sink you."

"What was the name of that ship we were looking for?" Pete asked, his voice gentle.

He heard Mike groan and then say, "The U.S.S. *Lollipop*."

"Well, she's right down below me, pardner." Mike's voice was low. "You sure, Pete?"

"Just about, Mike. She's old—there's twenty or thirty feet of coral on her in places. She's wood and—if you'll pull me up—I'll show you a dead-eye the likes of which haven't been seen in these parts for many a century."

Mike spoke bitterly as he began hoisting Pete again. "Oh, how I love a comic."

It was pitch-dark when Pete and Mike finished stowing the diving gear, switching oxygen bottles, and cleaning up the mess. All the time they had been talking, planning. Both of them were excited, but neither wanted the other to know it.

Pete went forward and began hauling up the anchor chain. Heaving, he broke the grapnel out and began feeding the chain down into the locker.

"Why don't we just stay here tonight and get an early start?" Mike asked.

"Let's don't take any more chances than we have to, Mike. Weber's in the Gulf somewhere chasing pips on his radar screen. He might come around here."

"Seems like a waste of time though."

"Not really. Up until about eleven it's too dark to work down there anyway. We'll slip back to the island and come back in the morning."

Pete started the engine, and the *Indra* moved slowly away.

"Hope that coconut doesn't pull loose," Mike said.

"We can find her again with the bearings. . . . What're the bearings of our fix?"

Mike rattled off the bearings.

"Good." Pete settled down at the wheel. "Mike, give us a week of fair weather and—we've got it."

"The gold?"

"Yep."

Mike didn't say anything for a long time as he just sat and looked into the darkness. Finally he said, "Pete, you know what's the first thing I'm going to buy if we find it?"

"A zoot suit," Pete said.

"Naw. A bicycle."

"Bicycle? How old did you say you were?"

"Look, meathead, what difference does that make? I remember that for a long time—for a whole lot of years—I wanted a bicycle, understand? I wanted one bad, and I never got one. So I'm going to get one. I'm going to get a red one with chromium all over it, and I'm going to ride it, see? After that, you know what I'm going to do?"

"I'm scared to guess," Pete said.

"Well, I'll tell you. I'm going to ride my bicycle down into the part of town I ran around in. I'm going

203

to ride it around down there until I see a kid—
just a young punk, see—who looks like he's want-
ing a bicycle as bad as I used to want one. Then
I'm going to give'm the red one and walk off,
see?"

Pete looked at Mike in the darkness. "Yes," he
said, "I see."

Cephalopod

The next morning Pete was again lying in the water on his back, gazing up at Mike on the *Indra*. The weather was beautiful with a featherlight wind which hardly ruffled the surface of the blue Gulf, and a cloudless sky which assured Pete that there would be more light sifting down to the *Santa Ybel*.

Pete looked up through the glass faceplate. He was in the heavy suit and could hear the faint

205

sound of the air pump working on deck. Mike looked small, Pete thought. He looked more like a very young kid than he had the day before. And Pete's life really depended on him now, for there was no oxygen bottle strapped on his back with this suit. It was entirely up to Mike to insure that the air pump continued to run; that the pressure of air coming down to him be steadily and correctly increased for each foot of depth; and that the volume of air be right all the time. Pete reflected on the gloomy distance he had to descend, and he felt sweat breaking out on his upper lip.

But he knew that he was wasting precious time just floating around on the surface, so he spoke into the microphone which was located to the left of the faceplate. "Is she steady?"

"Steady as a headache," Mike said.

"All right. Punch the clock, I'm going down."

Pete opened the outlet valve, and air whooshed out of the suit. The thirty-two-pound leads on his feet dragged them down; the forty pounds on his chest and back seemed to shove him. The suit deflated until he could feel it pressing in on him, and as he passed sixty feet, he felt dampness around the watertight rubber sleeve on his wrist. He closed the valve a little to equalize the pressure of air in the suit against the pressure of water outside.

As Mike called out, "Seventy feet," Pete said,

"Mike, as soon as I get on the bottom, I'm going to give you a description of what I see. Just in case."

"In case of what?"

"I don't know. But we should both know what progress we make. Maybe you'll have to do the diving."

"I'll dive anywhere as long as I can keep my head above water," Mike said.

Pete scooped with his hands against the water until he could look down.

Below him and to one side lay the *Santa Ybel*. She was encrusted with coral but, in the filtered sunlight, Pete could see the outline of her decks, the stumps where the masts had been, even the lumps of the guns lined up on her gun deck. He swam away from her with his hands and settled to the bottom thirty feet away. The black air hose came coiling down, startling him until he saw what it was.

"On bottom," Pete said. He looped the air hose and life line so that he would have some slack without the help of Mike and adjusted the valves. By letting air out or holding it in the suit, he could adjust the pressure until he could no longer feel the drag of the weights on his feet or feel the shoulder straps of the weights slung over his chest and back. By carefully adjusting the air he finally felt completely free in the water—neither pressed down against the bottom, nor having any tendency to float upward with each step.

This done, Pete looked slowly around. The sunlight came down pale and greenish through the water. A thousand small fish swam slowly around, sea shells crawled on the surface or lay with beautifully colored mouths wide open, feeding. Weird and lovely flowers which were actually living animals grew around the ship.

"Hit's right purty down here, pardner," Pete said. "Got a regular flower garden. I'm standing about amidships of the *Santa Ybel* and about thirty feet away from her. As far as I can make out, she is lying with her bow pointing almost due east. For about fifteen feet from amidships fore and aft the explosion which sank the submarine—or something—blasted away the thick coral that covers her and cracked it in long, jagged lines in other places. The coral has fallen down on the ocean floor in lumps and blocks. The coral, breaking away, pulled away the planking of her hull from just below the water line—anyway, what looks like the turn of the bilge—to the keel. . . . By the way, what's your air pressure?"

"Steady on fifty," Mike said.

"Volume?" Pete asked.

"Five cubic feet a minute."

"Fine. Hold both right where they are."

"Okay, fussy. How's about getting on with the treasure hunting?"

"Restrain yourself, lad," Pete said. Then he went on talking. "I'm going toward her bow now. . . . I'm close beside her, going around the bow. Those old Spaniards really believed in building tubs. She's round as a beer barrel forward. . . . Oops."

"What's the matter?" Mike asked, his voice anxious.

"Brother," Pete said, "I almost stepped off the edge of the world. Mike, you ought to see this. The ship is sitting right on the edge of a perpendicular cliff. I don't see how she stays there. . . . I'm going back to the stern now . . . back the way I came."

Pete turned around, being sure his hose and line were free all the time, and walked back down along the side of the ship. He skirted wide around the fallen coral and walked under the great overhanging cabin in which old Admiral Halivera had lived.

"Speak up," Mike said in a little while. "What's going on down there?"

"Just sitting here looking at all the sights," Pete said as he turned and went back to the middle of the ship. "There sure are some beautiful fish down here. Gold and blue and green, all sorts of colors with long strings and streamers."

"Listen, mate," Mike's voice snapped in the

speaker, "we'll take up nature study later. I want to see some of that gold."

"Keep your shirt on or I won't bring up a red bicycle," Pete said as he stopped in front of the place where the ship's side had been torn open. The great oak frames were so thick with coral that there was hardly space enough between them for a man's body to pass, and as Pete looked at them, they seemed to him to be almost like the bars of a prison.

With the sun overhead now, there were deep black shadows inside the frames.

Pete felt a little shiver sweep up his backbone. "I'm going in past the frames, Mike," he said quietly. "I'll have to stoop to get in so that's going to put a sharp bend in the air hose. Pay it out to me slowly as I pull."

"Inside the ship?" Mike asked.

"Yep. Through the broken place. . . . Let me have it." Pete felt the hose coming down, and he made a larger loop. Then, climbing carefully over the sharp, broken coral, he reached the ship. He measured the distance between two frames with one arm and found it wide enough to let him through if he went straight in. Sideways the chest and back weights, the light battery box, and the other equipment made him too wide. But he would have to stoop, or perhaps get down on his knees.

Very carefully, so as not to snag the rubber

and twill suit on coral or a barnacle, Pete inched his way forward and hunched his shoulders. Then, feeling above his head with his hands and finding nothing, he straightened up.

"Dark in here," he said. "Gloomy. I can't see but a few feet."

"Don't the light work?" Mike asked.

"I'm getting it now." Pete unhooked the 100 c.p. hand torch from the belt and felt back along the waterproof cord to the accumulator batteries in the box on his back. He found the switch, and the light went on.

"Works," he said. "But I'd rather have a good bright candle."

"I'll send one down," Mike said. "Do you want it lit or have you got a match?"

"Very funny," Pete said. He swung the light slowly from left to right. "I'm in a hold about twenty feet long, fifteen feet wide. Seems to be empty."

"No oxcart wheels?"

"Nope. There are two doors, one forward, the other aft. Both locked."

Pete reached around and got an iron-handled, small pickax out of the leather loop on his back. Moving slowly, pulling the line and air hose carefully into the room with him, he went to the forward door and studied the wide hasp and bolt, the ancient heart-shaped lock hanging down from it. Putting the point of the pickax behind it, he swung up, rocking against the lock. The old metal crumbled away.

"Lock's off. Now, does the door open?"

Pete pried at it with the pickax, and it fell from the hinges, floating slowly downward. Pete let it fall and then stepped on it.

"Door fell off. There's another room. Looks bigger than this one . . . and darker. I'm going in. . . . By the way, Mike, if I give you a quick signal to hoist away, don't jerk it. The hose is bent into the ship, and there'll be another bend at this door. Just a smooth, easy pull and if it stops coming smoothly, don't heave on it."

"Okay," Mike said.

"I'm inside the other room," Pete said in a moment. "Darker'n a Stetson hat. Only a few feet of the outboard bulkhead's off. . . . I wish I had a decent light! This thing penetrates about five feet."

Mike's voice was trembling a little. "Stop griping, for the love of Mike! *What's in there?*"

"Something," Pete said, slowly moving forward toward the shadowy shapes the small light showed. "Don't know what."

"Doesn't the gold shine?"

"Mike, everything down here is covered with gunk a foot thick," Pete said. "But there are shapes of things on the deck. Might be boxes or crates. I'll try one with the pickax. What's the time?"

"Twenty-eight minutes."

"Yipe! I'll have to come up in a little while."

Pete took three more steps into the gloomy room and put the lamp down on one of the vague shapes rising from the floor. He was about to raise and swing the pickax when a movement caught his eye.

For a moment Pete wasn't sure whether he had actually seen anything or whether it had been the shadow of a fish or even his own shadow. He wasn't even sure of the direction. With the pickax back over his shoulder, he stood perfectly still, looking carefully into the arc of light made by the torch.

Then he saw the movement again. Advancing slowly across the flat top of the object the light was sitting on was a thinnish, grayish line. As Pete watched, it flowed toward the light like a gray stream of molasses.

And it got thicker where it came over the edge, although the tip of it going toward the light was still thin and rounded.

For a moment Pete thought that it was some sort of underwater worm. He was on the point of ignoring it and going on with the downward swing of the pickax when he suddenly saw a second thin thing beginning to stream toward the light.

Pete lowered the pickax to the floor and then stood perfectly still. Slowly, picking out the mov-

ing streams in the black shadows, he followed
them back and saw at last a shapeless mass of
something only slightly less dark than the shadows. Peering at this, Pete then saw, and recognized, two pale yellow spots almost at the top of
the mass of shapeless gray.

"Mike," Pete said, almost whispering. "Mike!
Octopus. Hoist away. Hoist away!"

"Stand by," Mike's voice instantly replied.

As the line tightened, Pete reached out slowly
for the light.

He was too late. One of the flowing streams
slid up over the plastic lens, slid into the darkness
behind the case. As Pete moved slowly backward
toward the door, he felt a sudden hard jerk at his
back where the light cord went into the battery
box.

Then it was pitch-dark. Pete's knees went weak
and panic swept him like a hurricane. He wanted
to turn and run, to scramble out of the darkness
in which that horrible thing lived.

Pete, his stomach ice-cold and reeling, fear
drying his throat, stumbled over something and
would have fallen except for the steady pull on
the life line from Mike far above. As waves of
horror kept pulsing, Pete felt as though he could
not stand it down there; that he would have to
get out of the suit so that he could escape.

Then Mike's familiar, flat, ordinary voice

steadied him like a dousing with cold water. "Bear a hand, I'm hungry," Mike said.

Pete turned when he reached the area of light coming in through the broken place and squeezed back out on the ocean floor. Clearing his line and hose, he said, "All clear of the ship. Hoist away."

Then he could hear Mike talking to himself. "Down thirty-three minutes at one hundred and . . . and . . . eight feet. Thirty-three, thirty-three. Let's see . . . bring him up at twenty-five feet a minute. Stop him at thirty for four minutes. Then twenty for eight and at ten for thirteen minutes. Holy cow, half an hour before I can eat."

Then Mike said, "How big was the octopus?"

"Plenty," Pete said as he adjusted the outlet valve and started to rise steadily upward.

"Big enough to be dangerous?"

"Yep," Pete said.

"Do you think that's where the treasure is?"

"I wouldn't be surprised."

"Then we'll have to dynamite that rascal out of there."

Pete, without thinking, shook his head and banged one ear against the helmet. "Ouch," he said.

"What's the matter?"

"Bumped my head. . . . No dynamite."

"Why not?"

"Mike, the ship is absolutely teetering on the

edge of that cliff. I believe I could push it over
with a crowbar. If she goes over, she'll drop down
to a thousand feet . . . and that'll be the end of
the cartwheel."

Mike stopped hoisting, and Pete floated at
thirty feet below the surface. Through the suit
he could feel the difference in temperature already.

"What are you going to do then? Can you
snake the stuff out with the octopus in there?"

"Not me, brother," Pete said. "I'm not going
in there with him again. . . . He got the light."

"He did! Holy smoke, what are we going to
use for light?"

"Search me."

Mike's voice was disgusted. "Oh, what a mess!"

"Yeah," Pete said quietly. "A mess."

Mike began hoisting again, then stopped him
at twenty feet. Then for thirteen minutes at ten
feet. Pete paddled over close to the *Indra* and,
lying just under her, studied her bottom.

"The bottom's still pretty clean," he remarked.

"Come out from under there and talk to me,"
Mike said. "Are you just going to wait until that
octopus dies of old age?"

Pete paddled out from under the boat and lay
on his back looking up at the liquid silver of the
sea's surface.

"You look like an overgrown sausage down

there," Mike declared. "Can you see me? I'm waving my arms."

"Save your strength. The surface of the water is just like a mirror. But I can see myself beautifully. I look pretty good."

"How about taking an ax down and cutting off those arms?" Mike asked.

"There are eight of 'em. While I was cutting off one, the other seven would be taking this diving suit apart, probably starting at the air hose."

"How about that shark chaser? Maybe it'll chase him out of there."

"I'll try it. But I'm afraid it won't."

"How about some kind of poison?"

"Haven't got any."

"How about taking a wire down from the storage batteries? Hook one side to one arm and the other to another. Then I'd throw the switch and you could watch him fry."

"Haven't got enough wire. And who would do all the hooking up? That thing's arms are a good six feet long, Mike."

"Wow. How big around are they?"

"At the butt they're about the size of the main gaff."

"That big! How big do those things get anyway?"

"That's a statistic in which I'm only remotely interested," Pete said. "The one down there is big enough for me."

Pete's time was up, and Mike hoisted him to the surface. Pete climbed slowly up the little ladder over the stern and got on deck. Mike pulled the phone connection off and began unscrewing the helmet. As he took it off, he unconsciously pushed the "talk" button on his mouthpiece and said, "Well, what are we going to do?"

Pete patted him on the shoulder. "Remember me?"

Mike looked up and then grinned as he took the telephone off. Then he stopped grinning as Pete shucked out of the heavy, hot diving suit. "What are you going to do about that octopus, Pete?"

Pete didn't look up as he unlaced the weights from his feet.

"I don't know—yet, Mike," he said. "Right now that thing's got us licked."

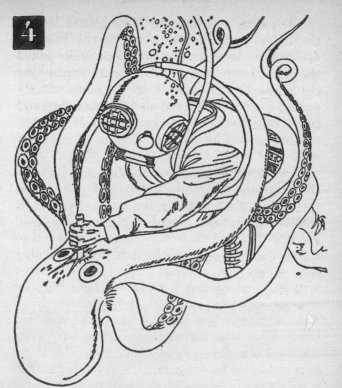

The Conflict Is Joined

Back in the lagoon, the *Indra* hidden behind the mangrove reef, Pete walked slowly along the sandy beach. The sun was going down into the calm western sea, the world seemed at peace. The things which made noise

219

by day became silent, and the things which made noise by night had not yet started. The only sounds were those the sea made against the white sand of the beach—a faint, liquid riffle—and the sound of the dying wind in the fronds of the coconut trees. There was also the noise made by Mike, who was trying to cut open a fresh coconut with a Boy Scout ax.

In Pete's mind there was no peace. As he walked slowly along, watching first one foot and then the other sink into the sand, he knew that there was only one thing for him to do. But he could not, yet, force himself to admit it. He could not stop thinking all around the one thing and go straight to it and think about it alone. The only way to get the octopus required an immense amount of absolutely ice-cold courage. Not the courage of men in battle when death is all around them, when there is no time to stop and think about whether you're brave or not, when there are other men close beside you. This thing Pete had to do took courage from the beginning, it would take courage all the way through to the end, and the courage would be a lonely thing.

So Pete took a long time while he tried to devise an easier way to kill the octopus. But at last he stopped walking, and he stopped thinking about easier ways, for there were none. There was only the one way.

He could not use any sort of explosion around

the *Santa Ybel.* The slightest jar might send her tumbling down the precipice. He had no poison. He doubted if the shark chaser would work, but he would try it first. He could make a long, sharp spear and stab the thing from a distance beyond the reach of its tentacles, but he knew that if he missed a vital spot, which was very probable, the thing would kill him.

There was only one thing to do.

Pete turned and went back down the beach. Mike was still whacking at the tough, fibrous green hull of the coconut. "I'll show you how to open one of those things," Pete said. "Sometime."

"Where you going?" Mike asked as Pete got into the boat and slipped the oars out.

"Be back in a little while," Pete said.

Aboard the *Indra* Pete got a one-volume encyclopedia and took it up to the cockpit. There was just enough light left to read by, and he found the entry "Octopus" and read it slowly and then read it again. One sentence stuck in his mind:

"The sucker-bearing arms, strong jaws, secreted poison, and sinister appearance of these animals have given them a name for ferocity which is not undeserved as their attacks on men are sufficiently well attested."

But, Pete thought, an octopus is only a cephalopod; it's kin to an oyster. It has a very small, rudimentary brain, and everything it does must follow a simple pattern of reflex action.

Pete shut the book and just sat looking vaguely at the island. In his mind he cleared away all other thoughts—as though sweeping debris from the floor of an empty room—and concentrated on the problem.

The octopus had a radula—a tongue—strong and sharp enough to tear through the twill and rubber of the diving suit. It had a paralyzing poison with which it killed its food. It had enormous strength. These were the things against which he must fight. These, and the fact that the battle would be fought far below the surface of the sea where he was dependent on an artificial supply of oxygen and would be greatly limited in his normal movements, whereas the octopus would be completely free.

What could he pit against these things? Pete thought. Compared to the strength of the octopus, his own strength was puny. There was no antidote for the poison once it was injected into him. He could not stop the radula from tearing his suit open if he got within range of it.

Pete had nothing but the mind of a human, a mind trained to think, to plan, to reason. A mind capable of foretelling the future by the events of the present and past. This was his only weapon. He knew a little about reflexes, about the behavior of animals, about the instinctive reactions of brains unable to reason.

With this weapon Pete planned his attack, established in his mind the pattern which would enable him to predict with accuracy what the octopus would do when confronted with a chain of circumstances which Pete would try to rigidly control and present to the animal.

As he rowed back to the beach, Pete remembered again the week-end leave he had taken on Hawaii, the Big Island. With a rubber-and-glass face mask he had gone swimming in the lava-strewn sea around Hilo and had come upon some Hawaiian boys spear fishing. They were marvelous in the water, and he had seen some of them swim down as far as thirty feet to spear an *uloa* or some other big fish.

And then one of them had found an octopus— a small one—in a crevice. Pete had watched the boy as he calmly reached into the crevice and let the octopus wrap tentacles around his bare arm. Then, swiftly, he had jerked the animal out and held it up above water.

Pete remembered his revulsion at the sight of the squirming, slimy, shapeless thing as it had writhed in the boy's grip.

Then the boy had put the octopus to his face— just for a second—and the thing died and became perfectly limp, the tentacles dangling.

Pete had gone over and asked him what he had

done to kill the thing so swiftly and the boy had showed him where he had simply bitten the animal close behind the pale yellow eyes, crushing the brain.

On the beach Mike had almost shucked the coconut and was sitting with it between his knees, scraping and pulling off the tough gray fibers. Pete, pulling out the Marine Corps combat knife, went up under the trees and got another nut and came back to sit beside Mike.

Without saying anything, Pete held the coconut, little end down, and swiftly whacked off green slices of the hull with the combat knife. Finally down into the white part, he took one more whack and sliced a clean round hole in the top of the nut itself. The sweet juice flowed slowly around the hole and Pete held it out to Mike.

"Boy, are you superior!" Mike said. "Know any more tricks?"

"Millions of 'em," Pete said, pulling a whetstone out of his hip pocket and a small can of oil out of his shirt pocket.

The double-edged stiletto blade of the knife gleamed almost gold in the dying light. Pete turned the seven-inch blade slowly over and looked at the scroll and the letters USMC on it. Then, with careful, slow strokes, he sharpened it.

The rest of that night was bad. Before they went to bed, he and Mike chatted a while, but Pete could not remember what they talked about.

In his bunk he listened to the soft lapping of the lagoon against the hull of the *Indra* while he fought back waves of fear which, in the darkness, tried to engulf him.

In the morning he did not tell Mike what he planned to do, because he knew that it would start an argument and he did not want to bother with that.

Pete waited until long past noon, for he wanted the sun to be in the western sky so that it would throw a little more light into the interior of the ship.

Then it was time to go down. Pete put on the self-contained suit, strapped the knife on the belt on his right side. Then he put on a pair of heavy, flexible rubber gloves. He did not want the octopus to be able to touch his bare skin anywhere, or to feel the warmth of a living being.

As Mike lifted the helmet, ready to lower it over his head, Pete said quietly, "Mike, I'm going to try to get the octopus. There's nothing you can do to help me."

"What do you mean?"

"Just that. Okay, put it on."

"Wait a minute, wait a minute," Mike said, lifting the helmet. "What's going on, Pete?"

"I've got it figured out. Put the helmet on."

The helmet came down. Pete could hear Mike screwing the connections on, snapping on the life line.

"One, two, three . . ." Mike said over the telephone.

"Five by five," Pete said in his microphone. "Lower away."

Pete looked up once at the silver surface of the water, broken by the hull of the *Indra*. Then, paddling, he went over to the black line of the anchor chain and held it lightly. Like sliding down the banisters, he thought.

On the bottom Pete adjusted the valves until he was featherlight, for he wanted the least possible resistance. Then into the mouthpiece he said, "Mike, I'm disconnecting the phone and the life line now. I'm snapping the end of the life line to the ringbolt in the anchor. I might need it again sometime.

"But if I don't, Mike . . . if you don't hear from me within an hour and a half . . . just . . . call it a day. Remember those numbers, and get someone else to help you get the stuff. It'll be here."

"Pete! Wait a minute. *Pete*, listen. . . ."

Pete unscrewed the watertight plug and heard the phone connection go dead. He unsnapped the life line and snapped it again on the ringbolt. Then he was completely free of any connection with the *Indra*.

"I feel naked," Pete said to himself as he stood looking at the life line and the bright brass prongs of the phone connection.

Then he turned and walked toward the *Santa Ybel*.

He squeezed between the encrusted frames and stood in the first room. The slanting sunlight lit it well, and it was empty.

Pete was sick and weak with fear as he walked slowly through the room to the gaping door of the next one. At the door he hesitated for a moment and then stepped, carefully, through the opening and to one side so as not to block the light.

He stood for a long time waiting for his eyes to become accustomed to the gloom. Gradually, as he waited, he again became able to see the boxes and crates and lumps piled on the floor of the room, and at last he was able to make out the back wall and the two side walls.

Then, on the floor he saw the empty shells of many mollusks—cockles, whelks, limpets, murices, cowries—and the empty hulls of crabs. And, lying in a space empty of objects he made out the bones of a man.

He had adjusted his buoyancy so that he almost floated as he walked, and now he took a step forward into the room. Then another. As he went away from the wall at his back, he felt lost and desolate. He took two more steps and reached a large, squarish lump crusted with sea growth.

And then—as though it had suddenly appeared there, and yet there had been no visible movement—he saw the rounded dome of the octopus and the hooded eyes, pale yellow with black slits, staring out at him from the darkness of the room with an intensity so baleful that he felt almost nauseated.

Pete stood perfectly still, the oxygen hissing quietly into the helmet. His mind was now cluttered with thoughts; utter loneliness was like a weight pressing down on him; uncontrolled fear moved in the pit of his stomach. He waited, trying to breathe slowly, until his mind cleared and became familiar to him, became the mind of a controlled man holding to a single train of thought, concentrated entirely and with complete detachment on the plan of attack.

Still standing still, Pete slowly ripped open the packet of shark chaser at his belt. The dye spread slowly through the room, seeping along the floor. He watched as it reached and flowed around the dome of the octopus.

The animal did not move.

Pete watched it for a long time as the dye slowly dissipated. He had known that it would not work. There was no escape from the thing he had to do.

He could now make out the camouflaged tentacles of the octopus extending into the room, long and the color of dead flesh as they lay motionless on the dead surface of the sea growth. With an almost imperceptible movement Pete drifted toward the thing as he watched the hateful eyes, watched the motionless tentacles. Pete was stooped over a little, the combat knife bare in his right hand, his left arm across his chest, his left hand under his right armpit.

The plastic lens of the underwater light gleamed pale on the floor and Pete glanced down at it. When he looked up again, he saw the tentacle to his left moving. Inside the sucker-lined sheath muscles oozed back toward the hood, and the butt of the tentacle began to swell and then, slowly and smoothly rising from the floor, the tip end of the tentacle came up like the head of a cobra. For long seconds it undulated gently and then began its slow approach toward his body.

Pete stopped every movement of his muscles except his slow and gentle breathing. Requiring the total power of his mind, he stopped the involuntary trembling of his knees, the quivering of his lower lip, the convulsive reaction of his stomach pressing up against his diaphragm. He knew that the time for flight was forever gone; the conflict had been joined.

He could not stop the slow closing of his eyes, the tremor of their lids, or the thick swallowing in his throat. When he opened his eyes, the tentacle was reaching out toward him, and he watched the thin, death-gray tip of it as it came. He saw the circular mouths of the rows of suckers, and as the tactile tip touched him, the sucker mouths opened and shut in a convulsive movement all along the tentacle.

Through the diving dress he could not feel the tentacle at all, but he knew that it was sliding around his body, for he could see at the edge of the faceplate the diameter of it, just below his left elbow, growing, swelling, and he could see the rows of suckers sliding past.

The implacable eyes stared, unblinking; the mantle of the thing then began to convulse slowly.

The faceplate of the helmet sharply defined the area of Pete's vision, and he was startled when he saw the tip of the tentacle appear again on his right side. The squirming end of the thing moved more swiftly now as it continued to encircle him just above the hipbones. As though it was blind, it felt its way along, searching in the folds of the diving suit, sliding over small summits and into the valleys of them.

Pete could still feel nothing through the heavy dress. The tentacle continued, the tip now disappearing past the left edge of the faceplate, the band of the tentacle across his belly swelling steadily.

Then Pete felt the pressure. Not suddenly, not with a jerk or a squeeze. It was just a slowly growing pressure around his waist, particularly against his back. There was no feeling of constriction, just of compulsion. It was as though a solid wall was behind him, pushing him forward.

Then, with horror, Pete suddenly realized that the tentacle had pinned his right arm to his side, pinned the knife against his leg. His mind stopped the almost instantaneous impulse to raise his arm, free the knife. He forced himself to become completely relaxed, offering no resistance whatsoever as the tentacle drew him with increasing speed toward the dome of the animal.

Pete turned his eyes to those of the octopus, and they stared at each other steadily. Pete tried to penetrate through the eyes into the mind of the animal which held his life encircled, while his own mind coldly calculated distances, pressures, the length of the razor-sharp radula which could slice open the dress and let the enormous crush of the sea in upon his body.

Now he must lower his left arm, move it down outside the grasping tentacle, move the hand down until the fingers could reach and replace those of his right hand on the hilt of the knife. The action must be so slow that the octopus would not interpret it as a threatening movement, so slow that to the yellow eyes it would appear to be only drifting, and yet the movement had to be completed before his body was drawn close to the hood and the rake of the radula; it had to be completed before, in the violence of the animal's gluttony, the thing should grab him with other tentacles, jerk him forward and clamp him against the mouth which Pete could now see, the folds of it working like a nest of snakes.

As Pete started the deliberate, snail-slow passage of his left hand downward, he saw another tentacle moving forward, saw the tip touch and slide around his legs and felt the new pressure. Then a third tentacle rose, the tip touched the faceplate an inch from his eyes, slid slowly over it until the small double row of suckers was oozing across the glass. In dread Pete watched as the area of glass through which he could see was slowly reduced by the swelling tentacle until almost all light was blocked and there remained but a slit at the bottom through which he could see only the underside of the tentacle, the suckers convulsing, and beyond, the yellow eyes.

The movement of his left hand continued, and with all his will power he forced his mind to remain as calm, detached, and concentrated as it would have been in the safety of the *Indra*. Estimating the diameter of the tentacle around his waist, he was careful not to let his moving hand brush it. Once, when he let his movements become too fast, he felt the instant reaction of the animal—a quick tightening of all the tentacles.

In the dim light now inside the helmet Pete could make out the round suckers working on the polished glass faceplate. First the lip would touch the glass in a thin, circular line, then it would flatten into a pale ribbon as the suction began, and finally the interior of the mouth would come down white and deathlike to ooze inside the motionless band of lip.

The fingers of his left hand touched the wrist of his right. The knife was so close now—if he bent his right hand up, he would be able to shift it with no further movement of his left hand. But he did not do it, for he knew that any movement of his arm inside the coil of the tentacles would result in instant and crushing pressure. Anything he did now which the octopus could interpret as an attempt to escape would certainly mean his death.

He could feel the little ball on the hilt of the knife, but his hands in the heavy rubber gloves were clumsy as the fingers slid slowly down against the fingers of his right hand.

The fear of dropping the knife was terrible as his fingers continued their controlled and dead-slow movement. He raised the first finger of his right hand, the finger of the left taking its place. He raised the second finger.

His time was running out. Through the slit of the faceplate he saw a sudden horrible change sweep over the octopus. From its dead gray a wave of color tinged its body, receded, and another wave, this one blotched with gray and purplish brown, took its place. The pressure of the tentacles increased; he could feel now the swift passage of his body toward the animal.

With the knife at last gripped in his left hand, his left arm slowly rising in a calculated passage between the tentacles which now held him, Pete was suddenly drawn in under the mantle of the octopus.

For a moment the animal held him so that the hooded eyes were close to his own. The tentacles across the faceplate oozed away, and suddenly Pete's whole circle of vision was clear again and he could look straight into the sinister and baleful eyes.

He knew now that the time of his life was being measured out in seconds, and yet he held back the desire, strong as panic, to stab into the eyes.

Pete continued the slow raising of his left arm.

The radula began to rake him, gently at first, the sounds of the teeth against the rough twill rasping.

Pete studied the two hoods containing the eyes. In the gloom of the room he calculated the distance behind them on the now slowly convulsing dome of the octopus. Above the dome the long knife gleamed, and a pale blue and golden fish swam away from it.

Pete recognized the spot the point of the knife must enter. It was small in area, and it was moving with the convulsions of the animal. To miss it would mean his death.

Pete fixed his eyes on the moving spot, and the downward thrust began.

At the first instant of the stab—as Pete's muscles tensed along his left side, flowed over his shoulder, and pulled downward—the tentacles crushed in around him, the radula raked across the twill suit, the suckers ripped at him. A tentacle, the tip of it moving so fast that it was only a blur of gray, seized his left wrist and he felt the shock of its strength.

Too late. As Pete's breath came crushing up out of his lungs in a short, harsh moan, as the radula flailed the metal helmet, the Marine Corps knife drove down seven and a quarter inches through the brain of the animal. A flood of ink shot from the octopus and the room was suddenly utterly dark.

Pete realized slowly that he had been unconscious for a while—how long he did not know. As he opened his eyes, he saw nothing except inky blackness. And there was an enormous weight pressing him down against the floor of the room.

Moving slowly, his body trembling, he pushed upward. The weight oozed off him and he stood up.

The ink slowly cleared until he could see the animal sprawled among the dim crates. The knife hilt made a dull silver line. Pete, revulsion tight in his stomach, reached far out and grasped the knife. It came away easily, blood oozing out from where it had been.

Then panic hit Pete. Turning, he ran through the door, crashed into the frames of the ship, staggered back and ran at them again, jamming his way out to the open floor of the ocean.

Then he heard his own breath dry and hard and he stopped running. He turned slowly, looked back at the ship from which the black ink of the octopus was still flowing, and then turned again and walked to the anchor chain.

His knees were weak and his hands were shaking so that he had trouble snapping the life line to his suit. It was a long time before he got the telephone plug in, but at last he screwed it tight.

"Mike." Pete heard his own voice, and it was only a whisper. "Mike. Bring me up."

"Roger, wilco," Mike's voice answered. It sounded cheerful. Pete sighed and slumped down on the white sand, waiting until the life line began hoisting him upward.

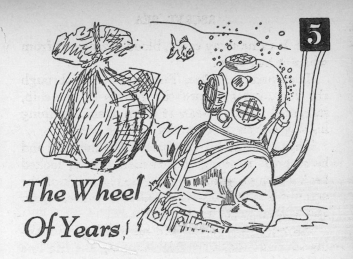

5

The Wheel Of Years

The sunset was again peaceful, the world calm as the *Indra* rode at anchor in the little lagoon. Pete, however, was not slowly walking along the beach dreading the encounter with the octopus. He and Mike were both in the main cabin working. Coils of rope had been brought aft from the forecastle peak, a small cargo net was spread out on the floor, in one corner Pete was collecting a small pile of tools.

Mike was measuring three-quarter-inch rope and coiling it down—measuring out thirty fathoms of it with a three-foot rule.

"How'd you kill that thing, Pete?" he asked.

Pete didn't look up from his examination of a six-point ripping saw. "Stabbed it."

237

"Just walked right up to it and stabbed it, eh?"

"Practically."

"Seventeen . . . eighteen . . . Don't give me that modest-hero stuff, Mac. What happened down there? It took you twenty-six minutes."

"That long?" Pete put the saw down on the pile of tools and began rummaging in a gear locker.

"Come on, give," Mike said.

"I just figured that the octopus had never seen a self-contained diver's suit," Pete said, pulling stuff out of the gear locker. "Figured he wouldn't know whether I was good to eat or not, or whether I was an enemy. So I walked right up to it."

"Yeah?"

"He wrapped two or three arms around me and I just relaxed."

"Ugh," Mike said, grunting.

"Since I didn't resist him, he decided I wasn't an enemy. So he brought me in close to see if I was good to eat. That's where he made the greatest mistake of his life."

Mike stopped measuring the rope and stood looking at Pete still rummaging in the gear locker.

"As soon as I was in close enough, I let him have it with the knife the Marines clean their fingernails with."

"Suppose you'd missed?"

Pete shrugged. "Would've been rugged."

Mike said slowly, "Brother, you took an awful chance. Weren't you scared when he wrapped those things around you?"

"Stiff," Pete said.

"I guess you were too busy to worry about ol' Mike, but those were the longest twenty-six minutes I ever put in," Mike said. "When you disconnected the phone and I didn't hear any more, there wasn't a thing to do but stand around on one foot and wonder what was going on. After twenty minutes I decided that the thing had got you. I was sort of glad to hear you gurgling again."

"You sounded pretty good yourself. 'Roger wilco.'"

Mike grinned. "You had that thing all figured out before you went down, didn't you?"

Pete nodded.

Mike started measuring rope again. "It would've been right lonely sailing back all by myself."

"I can imagine," Pete said. Then he held up a short rifle. "Ever shoot one of these hull thumpers?"

"Twenty-three . . . Is that a carbine?" Mike put the rope down carefully and stepped over it. Hefting the M-1 carbine, he said, "Boy, I bet that thing kicks the britches off you."

"Nope. Very sweet-shooting piece of artillery. Little heavy on the muzzle blast but no kick."

"How does she work?"

Pete got a clip of cartridges from the box and slipped them up into the underside of the receiver. Then he pulled the bolt back and let it ride home. "The safety's on the trigger guard— push her over and she's ready to go."

"How many bullets?"

"Fifteen in the clip and one in the gun. Semiauto, gas-operated. She doesn't ride up very much, so you can do a lot of perforating in a very short time."

Mike held the gun gingerly, looking at it. As Pete turned back to the gear locker, Mike laid the carbine gently down in the bunk against the outboard bulkhead.

"Here's what I'm looking for," Pete said, holding up a small pair of ice tongs.

Mike laughed. "Did anybody ever tell you you were a pack rat, Pete?"

"Never mind the remarks. I want to get that dead octopus out of there. I don't want a bunch of sharks gnawing away on him while I'm in there. So you're going to haul him up to the surface and set him adrift. Secure one of the empty gas tins to him so he'll float away and not come dangling back down my neck, see?"

Pete added the tongs to the collection of tools while Mike finished measuring the rope.

"That does it for tonight," Pete said. "Sack time."

Mike turned off the light in the main cabin and pulled the black curtains away from the hatch and skylights so that the cool night wind came sweeping into the dark cabin. As he and Pete went forward in the darkness Mike said, "What do you think, Skipper?"

"Hard to tell, Mike. I might have to break through a lot of bulkheads before I can get to where the stuff is. Might take three or four days yet."

Mike groaned. "I thought it was in the room with the octopus."

"Might be. There's something in there. Among other things there's a human skeleton."

"You know, Pete," Mike said slowly, "sometimes I think we're never going to find the stuff. We get closer and closer, but we don't ever find anything."

"We'll find it. Good night."

"Night, Cap'n."

In the morning as Mike steered the *Indra* slowly upwind toward the floating coconut, Pete said, "We'd better put a new nut on it tomorrow. That one's getting sort of waterlogged."

Mike nodded as Pete went forward and picked up the anchor. He dropped it overboard and came aft.

"You going down in the self-contained out-fit?" Mike asked.

"No. Time's too limited in that. Anyway, you ought to do some work."

"I'll remember that," Mike said. "When you start gasping for air down there, you'll hear me laughing."

Pete laughed as he snapped a slide to the life line and climbed into the heavy outfit. Mike got the air pump running while Pete arranged the pile of tools in the cargo net and secured the thirty fathoms of rope to it. "I'll put a fisher-man's knot in the life line. That way you'll be able to slide stuff up and down the line, and I won't have to hunt all over the Gulf for it. In an emergency give it a hard yank and the knot'll slip."

For a few minutes Pete waited with the helmet on, testing the incoming air, the outlet valve, and the phone. "Okay, lower away," he said at last.

Down on the now familiar bottom, Pete drew enough life line and hose to permit him to move freely inside the ship with the line secured by a slip knot to one of the frames. This done, he asked Mike to lower away on the tools.

As he spread his gear out carefully on the white sand bottom, he listened to the valves clicking smoothly up in the air pump, and occasionally he could hear Mike pushing the "talk" button on the phone.

"Sort of lonely down here," Pete said. "How about a few jokes? Maybe a song?"

"For crying out loud," Mike said. "He wants jokes. . . . What are you doing, just sitting down there watching the mermaids? Why don't you go to work?"

"It's a nice day down here. Sun's shining, clouds drifting by. There's a blue-and-gold fish right against the faceplate looking in."

"Get to work," Mike said.

With the ice tongs secured to the hoisting line, Pete once more squeezed between the frames and entered the first room. As he walked toward the black doorway, he felt the cold shiver run up his spine and felt the sweat breaking out on his lip again. "I hope that thing is really dead," he said to Mike. "I couldn't go through that performance again."

"Take it easy, hear?"

"Don't worry."

Pete again went into the other room and stepped away from the door. It was much darker than it had been the day before with the sun west of the meridian, and he stood a long time waiting for his eyes to grow accustomed to the gloom.

As the shapes of the crates and boxes began to form in the gloom. Pete at last saw one of the tentacles, now pale gray, lying almost at his feet. Cautiously, ready to retreat through the door, he touched the thing with the heavy lead weight on his foot. It did not react.

"I guess it's dead all right," Pete said.

"Good."

Pete walked slowly forward until he found the body of the octopus. Some small crabs were clawing at the slit the knife had made.

With the ice tongs spread open, Pete swung them down and forced one prong into the knife slit, scattering the crabs. Then he clamped the tongs shut. As he stepped back, he saw again the plastic lens of the light.

"I'm tying the light above the octopus, Mike. See if it's beyond fixing, will you?"

"Okay. Ready to go?"

"Hoist away." Pete stepped to one side as he felt the hoisting line tighten. The octopus began to slide slowly across the floor, gliding over the crates and boxes, its long tentacles streaming out behind the body. Even dead, the thing made Pete's stomach go weak.

Mike hauled it through the door, across the empty room, and out between the frames. As Pete saw its tentacles disappear upward, he said, "She's all yours and clear of the ship."

"I think I'll just keep it and drape it on you if you give me any more trouble," Mike said.

"If I ever see that octopus again," Pete warned, "I'll cut your share down to only a million dollars."

"I want to see the first dollar," Mike said. "What're you doing now?"

"Going out to get a crowbar and a chipping hammer."

Pete got the tools and went back into the dark inner room. The first crate he tackled was too much for him—he couldn't get through it—so he went on beyond it to a low, circular lump on the floor covered with marine growth. Slipping the crowbar under it, he prized up and the thing moved.

"I've found something I can move anyway," he said into the phone. He leaned the crowbar against a box and got the chipping hammer from the belt loop.

Swinging the hammer took a great deal of effort at that depth. After bringing it down with all his strength the water resistance was so great that the hammer struck with about the force of a six-months-old baby swinging a rattle.

"You might as well go home. I'll be here for the rest of the summer," Pete said as he rested.

"What are you doing? Look, Mac, if you don't let me in on what you're doing, I'm coming down there and whale the daylights out of you."

"Come ahead. But be careful you don't hit bottom when you dive overboard. It's only a hundred and ten feet deep."

"A wise guy," Mike said in disgust. "Come on, Pete. What's going on?"

"I'm trying to chip the crust off a round lump down here. But it's just like swinging a tennis racket through a barrel of glue."

Pete went back to work, and the effort took all his breath, so that he couldn't keep talking to Mike. At last he chipped away a half inch of the growth, but there appeared to be inches more of it. "Maybe it'd be better to haul this thing out of here and see what it is after we get it up there."

"Maybe," Mike said. "But I don't want to be hauling up all the useless junk in that ship. I'm just a growing boy and even that octopus was heavy."

"What'd you do with him?"

"Oh, he's playing around on deck."

Pete took another vicious swing with the hammer and kicked up a little whirl of dust which floated slowly away in the gloom.

When it was gone, something shone dull and soft where the hammer had fallen.

Pete stared at it and then bent low, so that the faceplate was almost touching, and looked at it. Then he touched the glowing spot with his finger. It felt smooth and warm.

"Mike," Pete said quietly, "we've found it."

"The gold?"

"I think so. . . . I'm almost sure. Send the line down."

"The line's down, dope. What does it look like?"

"A lump of rock."

"How do you know it's gold?"

"I don't. But I think it is. I chipped a place clear on it and it shines."

"Might be brass."

"Could be," Pete said. But, looking at the dull, glowing spot, he knew, somehow, that it was not brass. Suddenly, as he stood still, he thought of Johnny. We're almost to the end of the long road, Pete said to himself.

Outside the ship Pete got the saw and went slowly along the break in the planking, peering in between each frame. At the first frame after the bulkhead of the empty room he sat down on a lump of coral which had been blasted away and began sawing at the bottom of the frame.

It was very hard work and he had to stop frequently to rest. Mike kept demanding to see the gold, and Pete finally explained to him that he was cutting a hole in the side of the ship where the room was so that he could get the round thing out the shortest way and not have to drag it through the door, the empty room, and then upend it and roll it between the frames.

"You're panting like a yard dog," Mike remarked. "Do you want me to step up the pressure and volume?"

"Might try it," Pete said. "Feels like I haven't had a decent breath for five minutes. And send down a sandwich."

"Ham on rye and double malted be all right?"

Pete laughed and went back to work. When he had cut away all the frames clear of planking, he had a hole in the side of the ship about eight feet long and five high.

"I've got a hole in her. How long have I been down?"

"Thirty-six."

"Jeepers! That's about the limit. But I'll try to get the cargo net under it before I come up. Then perhaps we can snake it out after I get topside."

"It's been there a long time," Mike said slowly. "It can stay another hour or so if you want to come up now."

"I'll stay another four minutes. But give me a stand-by at thirty-nine."

"Okay."

Pete dragged the heavy net through the hole. As he prized up a side of the round thing, the effort made his breath rasp and he realized that he was close to the limit. He jammed the net under half the thing, then prized up the other side, pulling the net all the way under. As he roved the cargo hook through the corners of the net, Mike said, "Stand by—thirty-nine, Pete."

"I've got her and am coming up."

It took thirty-three minutes for Pete to make the ascent and when he finally got out of the diving suit he was too tired to do anything but sit in the cockpit and sweat.

"Want me to start hoisting, Pete?"

"Might as well. But I'm pooped."

"I can do it alone, maybe."

Mike went over to the boom and started hauling. "Coming easy," he said.

"Sliding across the floor. The tough part will be getting it through the hole."

"Jammed now," Mike said after he'd gotten fifteen feet of line on deck.

"Don't force it. Might part everything. I'll go back down in an hour or so."

"No. She's free again." Mike's voice was getting excited. "Anything else to stop her, Pete?"

"Don't think so." Pete was too exhausted to have much interest, and he didn't even look aft at Mike straining as he heaved in on the line.

"Halfway up," Mike said, taking a turn around a bitt and stopping to pant. "If this turns out to be a brass cannon, I'm going to jump on you."

"Best opportunity you'll ever have. I could hardly whip you now with both hands tied behind my back."

Mike snorted and went back to hauling.

"There she is," he said after a while. Then his voice dropped as he peered over the side. "Pete, that's nothing but a chunk of coral."

Pete pushed himself up with his hands and walked slowly to the rail. In the bright sunshine the round thing looked brown and shapeless as it lay half awash in the cargo net.

His feet dragging with fatigue, Pete went forward, got another line, secured the end to a halyard winch, and brought the other end over to Mike. "Jump down and make her fast."

Mike took a frog leap over the life rail, secured the line, and came hand over hand back to the deck.

Pete shuffled back to the winch, and as he began to crank the line in, he felt dizzy and sick with fatigue. As Mike grunted at the hoist and the cargo net rose slowly from the water, Pete said, "Forty minutes down is too long. For me anyway. Maybe it's all right if you're just admiring the scenery, but it's too long for steady hard work down there. After this, half an hour."

"Okay. You look sort of green around the gills."

"Let's get this thing on deck and call it a day, Mike. I don't want to go down again."

"Don't blame you. Okay, *heave!*"

At last they got the thing up to deck level and swung it with the boom in over the side and dumped it on the stern.

Pete looked at the lump without interest and went to the companion hatch. "I've got to turn in, Mike. Must be an old man. You take her back to the island, will you?"

"Sure. Turn in, Skipper. I'll bring you something to eat if you want."

"No. Thanks, Mike. Just rest my weary bones."

After Pete stretched out on his bunk, he began to wonder whether the chart of time down and decompression time coming up that had come with the diving outfit was right. If, he thought, I'm this shot after every time down, I'll collapse after a few days of hard work down there.

But his thoughts trailed off into sleep.

Pete was dreaming about the octopus, and when something grasped his shoulder, he came surging up out of the bunk ready to fight.

Mike backed away. "Take it easy, boy."

Pete grinned. "What's up?"

"Nothing. Only you've been asleep for five hours. It's almost sunset. How do you feel?"

Pete climbed down out of his bunk. "Fine. Back to battery. . . . We in the lagoon?"

"Been there. Think you can make it topside?"

"I feel okay, Mike, really. That nap did the trick."

"Well, come on up. I want to show you this brass cannon."

"No kidding," Pete said. "Is that what it is?"

Mike nodded.

Pete snorted. "Beat myself into a stupor for a cannon."

The sun was just sinking as Pete followed Mike

up into the cockpit. The first thing Pete noticed was the mess all over the stern of the ship. Bits and pieces and chunks of coral were scattered around, slime and wet dirt covered the teak planking, and a set of his best wood chisels was scattered around. Pete was beginning to frown when a ray of sunlight flashed up from the deck.

In the middle of the mess there was a solid disk.

Pete walked over slowly and looked down at it.

"Haven't got it all cleaned off yet," Mike said. "But you can make out some of the carving on it. See, right in the middle there's a guy's head. Looks like a big tongue flapping out of his mouth. Then those pointed things around it. Like a compass card—eight of them. And there's all sorts of carving all over it."

Pete stood in silence looking down at the glowing thing.

"Nobody would go to all that trouble to carve on a piece of brass, would they, Pete? Look, there're all sorts of houses and people's hands and animals. See, that thing looks like a goat's head and that looks like a snake. They wouldn't do all that on brass, would they, Pete?"

"It's a calendar, Mike," Pete said quietly. "Aztec. They called it the Wheel of Years."

"Is it brass, Pete?"

Pete got down on his knees in the mess and licked the bare metal. "No. Not brass."

"Then it's gold?"

Mike was looking up at him, and his face was different from the face Pete had grown accustomed to. There wasn't any belligerence in it any more, Mike's lips weren't set tightly together in almost a sneer, and his eyes looked big and deep.

"It's gold, Mike."

Mike went over and sat down in the cockpit. "The red bicycle," he said quietly. "With chromium all over it."

6

Mutiny

For three days, which to Pete seemed years, they worked like slaves. Pete, resting only between loads, made three descents a day, staying on the bottom thirty-five minutes each time. This kept him five minutes at thirty feet, ten at twenty, and fifteen minutes at ten feet, with a total ascent time of thirty-three minutes for each time down. Pete knew that he was dangerously close to collapse and that he was flirting with the "bends"

254

but, ever since he had stood and looked down at the golden Wheel of Years, Pete had had a strange sense of impending danger.

He didn't know what caused it, nor when it would materialize, but that first night he had said to Mike, "Things are going too smooth, Mike. I've got a feeling that everything's going to break loose in a little while."

For a moment Mike hadn't said anything, but at last he looked up. "So have I," he had said quietly.

"Maybe it's the weather," Pete had said. "Maybe this fine spell we've been having is going to wind up with a bang and we'll catch another storm. Or maybe the *Santa Ybel* is going to slide down the precipice. I don't know what it is, but I feel the threat of something."

"It's not the weather, Mac," Mike had said, "and the *Santa Ybel* isn't going anywhere. It's old Razorface. He's going to show up, Pete. I feel it in my bones."

For a moment Pete had stood in silence in the blacked-out cabin watching Mike cleaning the last of the marine growth from the Wheel of Years. Then he had nodded. "I think so, too. So let's get that stuff out of there as fast as we can, Mike. Then get the masts back in and get going."

"Suits," Mike had said. "But you've got the heavy end of it, Skipper. All I do is haul it up."

And—after three days—Pete could agree that

he had the heavy end. The job of moving the heavy crates and getting the cargo net under them and secured so exhausted him that the sound of harsh, rattling breathing in the helmet seemed almost a normal state of affairs. And when he stood, shaking with fatigue and dizzy with it, and watched the hoisting rope snaking the stuff out through the hole he often thought that he could not move another muscle.

After the third day the topside of the *Indra* was piled with crates. At first Mike had opened them, prying open the heavy iron chests or breaking off the hinges, or splintering the heavy wood. But he soon stopped, for it was hard work and the reward was always disappointing, for the treasures inside were scummy and tarnished black. Just lumps in a bed of ooze. And he didn't have time to bother.

On the third day Pete watched a big crate slide slowly toward the opening and then turned away from it to swing the repaired light slowly around inside the room. The sun was so far down that, outside the cone of light, the room was dark. The bones of the man showed dull as ivory. The empty mollusk shells had been crushed by the movement of the heavy crates. Pete advanced slowly and, for the first time, noticed a roughly square hole through the bottom of the ship. He stooped to examine it and then looked curiously at the skeleton lying close to it. The light brought out the shape of something among the bones and Pete picked it up and looked at it more closely. It was a long knife with a gold hilt encrusted now with growth.

That man whose bones now littered the floor had sunk the ship, Pete decided. He remembered the writing in the log of the *Santa Ybel*. The weather had been fair, the ship sailing full and by, and suddenly, without explanation or apparent cause, she had started to sink. Pete turned the knife slowly in his hands and wondered at the strength of the man who had deliberately cut open the bottom of the ship. He wondered, also, if Uemac had known before he started that he was going to die when he finished opening the ship to the sea.

But now the room was empty. As Pete turned slowly back to the hole in the side, which made a dim, glowing square, he began planning how to get into the rest of the ship. In the middle of the overhead of this room was a hatch, closed and, Pete was ready to bet, battened down tight. Around the rest of the ship, only cracked in places by the explosion of the depth charges, was a wall of coral twenty feet thick.

Pete decided that he would have to start cutting through one of the walls of this room and he dreaded the effort he knew it would take. He also dreaded the thought of finding another octopus waiting for him in the next hold.

"That's all there is, Mike," Pete said. "This hold's empty. Start me up."

"Can you wait a minute, Cap'n? I haven't got this last lump on deck."

"Sure."

Pete crouched and went out through the opening and then sat down on one of the lumps of coral. In the faint and dying light he watched the schools of small fishes swim in and out of the range of his vision. Pete had noticed long before that fish were not afraid of him as long as he was completely under the water. They were even curious and would come up and press against the faceplate, peering in at him with their big, unblinking eyes. But if he was half in and half out of the water, they would not come anywhere near him.

"Okay, Pete, Ready?" Mike asked.

"Hoist away."

Pete floated gently up and came to a stop at thirty feet below the surface. Generally, on the ascent, Pete would just hang motionless in the watery space and his mind would go almost blank as he waited for the minutes to pass, but this time his mind did not go blank.

The feeling of danger was, suddenly, very strong—much stronger than it had been before. It made him feel helpless and angry because, not knowing what the danger was, he could not do anything about it.

"I believe we've got it all, Mike," he said.

"What makes you think so? There's a lot of space you haven't gotten into yet."

"I know. But suppose you were loading a ship: would you fill a hold half full and then go to another one? Or would you fill it full first?"

"That gold's heavy, Mac. They might have used it for ballast and scattered pieces of it all over the ship."

"Maybe so, but I don't think so," Pete said.

Mike hoisted him another ten feet and stopped him again.

"Here's something to think about, my sawed-off friend," Pete said after a while. "Weber doesn't know it yet, but he doesn't have to look for the *Santa Ybel* any more. All he has to find is the *Indra*."

"I thought of that one a week ago," Mike said.

"All he's got to do is catch us, back us against a wall with that pistol he's so fond of, and unload the stuff we've got on deck. And sail silently away into the sunset."

"You're a mental giant," Mike said.

"So, until we get under the protection of somebody a lot more powerful than Weber, we're hot as a fox."

"Want me to send down paper and a pencil so you can draw me a picture?"

Pete ignored him. Thinking out loud, he said, "Suppose we get the masts in and sail out of here tomorrow. We head for Miami. We'll have to go through the Straits, won't we? All right. Weber figures that we know where the *Santa Ybel* is. He can count days on his fingers and figure that we've found her and raised the treasure. With his little radar he can sit in the Straits, fanning it, and as soon as we enter—pounce."

"I hadn't thought of that," Mike admitted.

"So, instead of going to Miami, suppose we head for New Orleans? What happens? We've already found out that Weber is not a jughead. Suppose he has some stooge posted outside New Orleans? Outside Tampa? Outside everywhere. All with radars fanning a hundred-mile circle. In other words, now that we've got it, what are we going to do with it?"

Mike said slowly, "We've got to take a chance. We've got to pick out a port and take a chance on slipping in."

"I guess so."

Mike hauled him up to ten feet and stood leaning over the rail looking down at Pete floating idly in the water.

"I'd give that Wheel of Years for that old PC boat I had," Pete said. "Just one man on the twenty millimeter and Weber could sit in that black sloop and cry his little eyes out."

"Forget it," Mike said. "You're not in the Navy now and there isn't any PC boat. . . . Comin' up."

On deck Pete stripped off the suit and put it on the drying rack. Down in the cabin he tripped on something and almost fell with the helmet. He went back, turned on the light, and saw that he had tripped on the deadeye he had brought up from the *Santa Ybel* the first day. Hanging up the helmet, he picked up the deadeye and put it on one of the shelves.

Back on deck, Mike had the motor going, and Pete turned the *Indra* toward the lagoon. Looking at the ungainly crates and lumps of stuff on deck, already smelling like a fish factory as the sun rotted the growing stuff, Pete said, "Mike, I hadn't really thought about it before but there are millions of dollars worth of stuff in those stinking things."

"Well, *I've* been thinking about it," Mike said.

Pete said quietly, "There's enough money there for people to kill each other about, Mike."

"For crying out loud! You aren't threatening a little, tiny boy like me, are you? Because if you're planning to bump me off—just forget it. I'll beat you to a pulp."

Pete smiled a little. "I was thinking about Weber. If he ever sees that stuff, our lives won't be worth a dime."

"I know it. And . . . I believe he's right around here, Pete."

"So do I."

"Pete," Mike said, "did you ever have one of

those dreams about being in a great big empty room not bothering anybody and all of a sudden you notice the room looks smaller? Then you keep watching, but you don't see anything except that all the time the room's closing in on you, the walls coming closer and closer?"

Pete nodded. "I know what you mean." Pete hit the wheelbox with his fist. "I wish we *knew* something! Or there was something we could really fight."

"Yeah," Mike said.

Then they sat in silence, the sun setting behind them, the sea now soft and deep purple.

With a sudden movement Mike yanked the motor out of gear.

"What . . ."

"Hold it! Hold it!" Mike said. Then, almost whispering, he said, "Look in the lagoon, Pete."

Pete looked and saw the stubby mast, then the deckhouse, and finally the squat hull of a ship.

"What is it?"

As the *Indra* lost way, Pete got out the binoculars.

"It's a Diesel-engine job. I can see the stack. Looks like a commercial fish boat. She's the . . . B-O-N . . . *Bonita* out of Los Arroyos, Cuba. She's sighted us. I see a man on the stern shading his eyes."

"And," Mike said slowly, "he's tall and thin and's got a face like a razorback hog."

"Nope. He's a short, fat Cuban."

"Well, what's he doing in there?"

"I hope he's just lying up for the night."

"One'll get you ten he's one of Weber's stooges," Mike said. "Weber's ditched that black sloop and is probably peeking out of a porthole at us."

Pete didn't answer as for a long time he examined the boat with the glasses. Then he said slowly, "No, Mike. I don't think so. There's no sign of a radar antenna on that boat, and I don't think Weber would sail around without radar."

"Well, what are we going to do? Just lie out here all night?"

"Haul off," Pete said. "No use letting those people, whoever they are, sight this cargo. Slip her back in gear."

"Won't it look suspicious for us to come right straight for the island and then, as soon as we see that boat, turn around and haul off?" Mike asked.

"You're right." Then Pete suddenly clapped Mike on the back. "Mike, that's the answer to a prayer. Let's get the tender in the water."

"Hold up, sailor. What're you going to do?"

"Go in and talk to the Cuban."

"What about?"

Pete grinned. "Wait and see, my friend."

Mike looked at him in ominous silence and then went forward to unlash the tender. Pete helped him, and they lowered the fourteen-foot boat down into the water.

"Just hold her here until I get back," Pete said as he yanked the pull rope of the inboard engine.

Mike was still silent as he nodded. The expression in his face was curious, but Pete did not look up at him as the little motor started and he headed in toward the lagoon.

The Cuban captain, who spoke good English, welcomed Pete aboard and told him that he was looking for turtles. He explained that they caught the female turtles when they came out on the sandy beaches to lay their eggs. He was careful to add that they waited until the turtle finished laying her eggs before they caught her.

Pete made up a tale about how he was fishing for marlin, and soon he and the Cuban went below. Pete looked curiously around in the ship and asked the Cuban to show him all of it. The man was very willing, and Pete made sure that, except for two colored men, no one else was aboard.

On deck again, Pete explained that his ship drew too much water to get into the lagoon. The Cuban complained that he had found no turtles.

Then Pete asked him if he would take Mike back to Los Arroyos that night. "We're about out of provisions," Pete explained.

In five minutes everything was ready. Pete promised to pay the Cuban fifteen dollars to take Mike to the mainland and bring him back.

Aboard the *Indra* Pete said jubilantly, "Mike, our troubles are over. He's going to take you to Cuba. Where's some paper and a pen?"

Pete was halfway down the companionway when Mike said quietly, his voice ominous, "Wait a minute."

"No time to waste," Pete said, going on down the ladder.

Mike walked across the cockpit. "I said, 'Wait a minute.'"

The tone of his voice stopped Pete, and he looked back up the ladder. Mike's face looked pale, his eyes were glittery and hard, and his jaw set.

Pete came slowly up the ladder. "What's the trouble?" he asked quietly.

"Aren't you forgetting something, wise guy?" Mike asked, the words grinding out between his teeth.

"What?"

Mike swung his arm slowly, pointing to the dark shapes on the deck of the *Indra*. "That," he said.

"What about it, Mike?"

"Part of it's mine," Mike said in a low voice.

"Sure it is."

"So . . . I'm staying right where it is. You thought you were a pretty smart cooky, shipping me off to Cuba, didn't you? You thought you could just rush me into it, didn't you? 'No time to waste,' you said."

Mike's fists were doubled at his sides, and his lower lip was quivering. His eyes looked hard as steel balls, Pete thought.

"A wise guy. Get rid of me and sail away," Mike said. "Well, it won't work."

Pete went slowly over and sat down on the coaming of the cockpit. As he began to understand the meaning of what Mike had said, he was first angry and then, when that died, he was sad.

"Mike," Pete said, "you don't trust anybody, do you?"

"No, I don't," Mike said, his voice flat. "Why should I?"

Pete felt suddenly dog-tired, whipped. All the elation he had felt coming back from the Cuban's boat was gone. "Oh, I don't know," he said slowly. "People have to trust each other."

"Yeah? Where are the people who trusted Hitler?"

"A lot of 'em are dead," Pete said.

"Where are the people who trusted that yellowbelly—what's his name—Tojo? Where're they?"

"A lot of them are dead, too."

"Okay. I don't ask anybody to trust me and I don't trust anybody. So I'm not going to Cuba. Understand?"

Pete nodded slowly. "Okay, Mike," he said quietly.

Pete went slowly to his cabin, changed his clothes, and came back topside. It was almost dark, and Mike was sitting, doing nothing, on the wheelbox.

"Take care of things," Pete said quietly. "As soon as she pulls out, you might as well slip into the lagoon and anchor."

"Where are you going?" Mike asked.

"Cuba," Pete said.

"What for?"

"I think it would help."

"You're leaving me here . . . by myself?"

Pete nodded.

"You leaving the stuff?"

Pete nodded again.

There was just enough light left for Pete to see Mike's eyes. For a long, long time he and Mike looked at each other, neither of them blinking, neither shifting the point of his gaze. And then Mike's eyes went down for an instant, came back up again, and then slid on up far above Pete.

"Skipper," Mike said.

Pete waited.

Mike got down off the wheelbox and turned around so that his back was toward Pete. He cleared his throat a little and said, "Guess I ran off the beam, didn't I?"

"For a little while," Pete said.

Mike turned around again but didn't look up. "What do you want me to do in Cuba, Cap'n?"

Pete let his breath out slowly. Inside he began to feel good again. "I'll write out a message. See if you can get it radioed, Mike. Then get some odds and ends of groceries because I told my Cuban friend I was sending you for provisions. And give him this fifteen bucks."

"Okay," Mike said.

Pete went below and wrote the message while Mike changed into clean dungarees.

"Tell the captain that if he can get you back here by day after tomorrow it'll mean another five dollars," Pete said.

"Okay," Mike said. He swung a leg over the life line and got down into the tender. As Pete threw the painter down to him, Mike said, "Pete?"

Pete looked down at him standing in the bow of the boat, which was now drifting slowly away from the *Indra*.

"Yep?"

"How's about just forgetting what I said a while ago?"

"Don't remember a thing, Mike."

"Okay, I'll be seeing you," Mike said, and started the little engine.

Within half an hour Pete saw the running lights of the Cuban boat move out of the lagoon.

He thought he saw a small, dark figure in the bow of the ship waving. But the moon wasn't up and there was only starlight in the sky.

Pete nosed the *Indra* through the channel and dropped anchor close alongside the anchored tender. Then, with the motor stopped, he stood alone in the cockpit.

The feeling of danger, like the room of Mike's dream, was coming closer and closer.

Sugar Option Sugar

It was hot and muggy in the "Telegráfico," and a fly kept trying to light on Mike's nose as he waited for the telegraph operator to read the message Pete wanted sent.

The operator, a sweat-soaked handkerchief around his throat, finally looked up at Mike. He said in slow English with a heavy accent, "No onderstan' dees, señor. Can it not be translate een Spanish?"

"Translate een Spanish," Mike said. "Listen, *amigo*, I can't even translate it een Eenglis. Just send it the way it reads."

The captain of the boat, who had come along with Mike, talked with the operator for a long time, but at last the operator sighed and began working the bug on the table. Slowly he sent Pete's message to the cable center.

The address was: Wild Bill Williams, Barwick Hotel, Miami, Florida, and the message read:

MAYDAY REPEAT MAYDAY XRAY POINT OPTION EIGHT FIVE DASH FIVE SEVEN DASH ZERO SIX NEGATIVE TWO ONE DASH FOUR EIGHT DASH ONE ZERO WILLIAM XRAY DOG DAY NINETEEN HOW HOUR SIXTEEN HUNDRED XRAY WATCH FOR WINDOW XRAY WAIT FOR BABY.   PETE MARTIN

"Eet iss trahnsmit, señor." He sounded sad.

"*Muchas gracias.*" Mike paid him and went out, the captain at his heels.

Mike stood beside the Cuban captain and watched the little island coming up green and round as dawn began to glow in the eastern sky. As the potbellied ship came around the point, Mike saw that the lagoon was empty. And as far as he could see across the dark water of the Gulf, it was empty, too.

"Where is your *amigo?*" the captain asked.

"He's around," Mike said. "Hove to some-where."

"It is the day he said," the captain remarked. "There was mention of five dollars."

Mike peeled off five one-dollar bills from the thin roll of money Pete had given him. "Thanks very much."

"*Por nada*," the Cuban said. "Do you wish to be left on the island?"

"Yeah," Mike said. "That's what I wish. Just maroon me, *amigo*."

The captain thought that was funny.

In the lagoon the two hands rowed Mike and his groceries ashore. They waved to him as he stood alone on the beach.

Mike watched the Cuban boat chug slowly out through the channel and turn east. The sun pulled its rim out of the clinging sea and seemed to bounce up a little way into the sky.

Mike looked down at the tin cans of food shining bright and clean in the new sunlight. "And I haven't even got a can opener," he said aloud. Then he looked again at the empty sea. Slowly he doubled up his fists. "Boy, am I a sucker," he said between his teeth. He turned his head slowly and looked at the small curving beach, the scattered trees green in the sunlight, the scraggly bushes. "Marooned is right," Mike said.

Then he heard the faint exhaust of a motor and at last saw the *Indra* nosing slowly around the western end of the island, Pete standing up at the wheel. It came in through the channel and Pete dropped the anchor with a white splash. He was towing the tender and soon came ashore.

"Boy, I thought you'd copped the gold and left me," Mike said.

"Fly right," Pete said. "Did you get the message off?"

"If that's what you call a message, yes."

"Good. Now let's get moving, Mike. I've got the masts all ready to step."

"Oh, my aching GI back. Have we got to haul those things up again?"

Pete nodded. "We'll get 'em in and then go back to the *Santa Ybel*. I'll cut through into the rest of the ship and, if we don't find anything, we can get away that much faster. Don't you think so?"

"Sure. Okay, let's strike a blow for liberty," Mike said, peeling off his shirt.

They got into the tender and went out to the ship. Pete followed Mike aboard.

"How about we eat some——" Suddenly Mike stopped. He whirled around to face Pete. "Listen, Mac," he said, "where's the stuff?" For the deck of the *Indra* had been cleared, all evidence of the treasure had disappeared, and the deck had been swabbed down.

Pete pointed down with one finger.

Mike went to the companion hatch and peered

down into the cabin. He whirled around again. "No tricks. Where is it?"

Pete beckoned with his finger and grinned. Mike walked slowly forward.

Pete pointed down into the shallow water. "Right down there," he said.

Mike stared into the water. He could see fish swimming around and a shell crawling along the smooth, sandy bottom—but that was all. "I don't see it, Mac," he said.

"See those four conch shells? They mark the square," Pete said. "I don't want to be boastin' an' braggin', but I think that's a good job of hiding."

"Yeh. It is if it's really down there."

"It's there, Mike," Pete said quietly. "All of it."

Mike looked at him for a long time. Then he looked away. In a low voice he said, "I guess I went to school too long. That school with the wall around it."

Pete didn't answer as he went forward to get the anchor up.

Over the *Santa Ybel* again, Mike dropped anchor. When he came aft, Pete was bringing the heavy suit up out of the cabin. Mike went over and started the air pump. "Pete," he said, "how's chances of letting me go down once? All I've done is stand around."

"You want to?"

Mike nodded. "I'd just like to see what it looks like. I don't want to stay very long. How's about it, Skipper?"

"Climb in," Pete said, holding the suit open. As he laced Mike into the suit, he gave him instructions, and when he finished and lowered the helmet, Pete said, "Good-by."

Mike pushed the helmet away. "What do you mean, 'good-by'?"

"Nice knowing you," Pete said, and put the helmet on.

He connected the phone and said, "One, two, three . . ."

"Five by five." Mike's voice sounded a little shaky, Pete thought.

"Don't forget that outlet valve as soon as you get in the water, Mike," Pete said.

"What do you think I am, a dope, dope?"

"Pardon me," Pete said. "Plenty of air? Feel okay?"

"Fine! Let her go."

"If you see any sharks, rip loose that shark chaser at your belt."

"Roger. How do I look?" Mike tried to walk and almost toppled over as the lead weights held his feet planted on the deck.

"Sharp. Like a sack half full of potatoes. Okay, here you go."

Pete lowered him down to the surface of the water.

"Think I'll just lie here a while and get used to it," Mike said, lying on his back and looking up through the faceplate at Pete.

"If you're going down, go on."

"Look, who's running this operation?"

"Nobody. How about that outlet valve?"

"I'll take care of the outlet valve. You just stick to your tatting, bub."

Pete waited, watching for bubbles to come out of the helmet, but none did. Slowly, as Mike failed to open the valve, the air inside the suit began to blow it up. The wrinkles unfolded out of the rubbery legs, then the back began to puff out.

"What's the matter?" Pete asked. "Scared?"

"Who, me?"

Pete could see Mike's face glaring up at him from the helmet.

Then the air filled out the suit completely, snapping the arms straight out so that the whole suit was stiff and round. Pete began to laugh.

"What's so funny?" Mike asked.

"You. How about that outlet valve, friend?"

"Okay."

Pete watched as Mike struggled. It was useless. The air inside the suit kept the arms stretched straight out so that Mike was helpless.

"What's got me?" Mike asked, his voice shaking a little.

"Nothing. Now you know what the inside of a balloon feels like."

"Say, what's going on? I can't move!"

Pete hauled him up until he could reach down and turn the valve. Air gushed out, the suit collapsed, and he let Mike sink straight down for about fifteen feet. Mike began to yell, and Pete hauled him up again.

"Do you or don't you want to go down?"

He could hear Mike gulping, but then he said, "Yeah. I guess so. Yeah, go ahead, Pete."

Pete let the life line go on the run and Mike plummeted down, leaving a trail of bubbles.

"Whoops! Where am I?"

"Halfway."

"You're not dropping me into that thousand-foot hole, are you? It's awful deep down here."

"It gets deeper."

"Hey!" Mike yelled. "Lookit the fish. He swam right past me, Pete. I could've caught him with my bare hand."

"Try it."

"How much further?" Then Mike grunted as he hit bottom. Pete waited for him to say something but all he could hear was Mike's breathing.

After a while Pete said, "Mike? You okay?"

Mike's voice was almost a whisper. "Yeah. Yeah, Pete. . . . Boy, it's sure pretty down here. Looks like walkin' around in the middle of moonlight. And the fishes and flowers and everything. I never saw anything like this. . . . Well, look at that. When I reached for that flower, it just went back inside itself, Pete."

"Sea anemone. It's alive."

"Well, blow me down. . . . Is that big gray thing the *Santa Ybel?* . . . Yeah, I can see the frames now. She looks sort of grand, doesn't she, Pete? Sort of lonesome, too. Okay to go inside her?"

"Watch your hose and line—keep 'em clear of stuff."

"Dark in here," Mike said. "Gloomy. Where was the octopus?"

"See the skeleton? Over to the left of that."

Pete watched the second hand of the stop watch clicking steadily around the dial. A sea gull flew over the ship, and Pete looked up at it. It had a broken leg which hung down, while the other one stayed tucked up. It hovered above Pete, looking down at him with its hard, bright little eyes.

"Pete," Mike said after a while.

"What?"

"Let's leave her alone."

"Leave what?"

"The *Santa Ybel*. Let's don't cut her all up, Pete. We've got plenty, don't you think?"

"Yes," Pete said.

"No use cutting holes all in her, is there, Pete?"

"I don't think so, if you don't."

"Let's leave her alone."

"Okay."

"You suppose she'll last another four hundred years?"

"Easy."

"Boy, it sure is lonesome down here."

Pete caught the flash of the sea gull's wing out of the corner of his eye and turned to look at it.

Below the sea gull, resting on the sharp blue curve of the horizon, was a narrow white triangle. Pete grabbed the binoculars out of the compartment and swept the sea with them.

Then he stood perfectly still, the binoculars dangling from the neck strap, the stop watch dangling from its chain. Slowly the muscles along his jawbones began to stand out, and then he clamped his lips shut.

Stooping, he took a bearing across the compass on the triangle of sail and checked the time on the stop watch. Mike was talking about a red-and-yellow fish he was looking at, but Pete didn't hear him.

Pete stooped and took another bearing. There was no change; the sail was coming straight toward the *Indra*.

"Mike. Here they come."

"Who?"

"Weber."

Mike yelled, "Get me up out of here. Get me up!"

"Take it easy. I think it's Weber. It's a Marconi-rigged sail. I can see the top of it, and it's coming straight for us."

"I want to come up," Mike almost wailed.

"First find the grapnel. It's over behind that big chunk of coral. Unshackle the wire from it and let the coconut go adrift. Bear a hand."

"I'm standing right beside it. . . . It's free."

Pete looked forward and saw the coconut begin to drift slowly southward.

He ran forward, weighed anchor, and left it dangling as he ran aft again and got the engine started. Shifting into reverse and taking the becket off the wheel, he steered the *Indra* backward straight down toward the growing triangle of sail.

"I'm under way, going astern slowly. Stand by to come up to thirty."

"Stand by! I'm waiting."

Steering with both bare feet, Pete hoisted Mike up to thirty feet and left him there for one minute, then pulled him to twenty.

"Do you itch anywhere?" he asked.

"I take a bath every Saturday, bub."

"Let me know if you itch. Around finger or toe joints. This is no time to get the bends."

"I don't itch," Mike said.

After five minutes Pete hauled him up to ten feet and could see him streaming out forward as the ship moved steadily astern.

Pete put the binoculars down and said quietly, "It's the black sloop, Mike."

"What do you think's going to happen, Pete?"

"They'll get rough," Pete said. "Time's up." He shifted into neutral and hoisted Mike on board and helped him out of the suit.

Mike stood for a moment looking at the sloop. "If I hadn't been such a jerk and gone down to see the sights we could have slipped away early this morning."

Pete shook his head. "No. I think Weber picked us up last night."

Mike went over, turned off the air pump, and carefully put the tarpaulin on it. When he came back to stand beside Pete, they could see the figures of people moving on the black sloop.

"You've got to hand it to Weber," Mike said. "He's a plenty smart cooky."

"He's still got a piece of work to do, though."

Mike grunted. "How about the carbine?"

Pete shook his head. "First place, they've probably got machine guns. In the second, they can't find anything aboard the *Indra*. So let 'em come."

"Nice day for a kicking around," Mike said.

"Couldn't be better. What time is it?"

Mike went over and looked at the clock. "Seven bells."

Pete stopped the engine and went below. When he came topside, he had a cloth bundle wrapped with light twine stops. He snapped it to the flag hoist and hauled it up to the main topmast peak. Then he secured the downhaul to a cleat beside the companion hatch.

"What's that? The laundry?"

"Another message. If we get a chance to use it."

"I hope it makes more sense than the first one."

Pete looked aft at the sloop. "We've got about twenty minutes before things start popping. How about a little chow, Mike? I think we'll need it before the afternoon is over."

"My throat's so dry now I couldn't eat," Mike said. "But I might as well try."

Mike came up in a few minutes with some of his dripping sandwiches and a pot of warmed-over coffee.

As Pete ate and watched the sloop, he said, "Mike, this is going to be a rugged affair. The Nazis learned how to get pretty nasty."

Mike looked over the edge of his sandwich and nodded.

"But it isn't going to last forever—I hope. So take it if you can."

Mike swallowed a hunk of sandwich and looked at Pete. "The Nazis don't know a thing we didn't know in the reform school," he said belligerently.

"Remember, Mike. Weber doesn't know where the stuff is. We do. As long as we can keep it that way, he can get just so rough and no rougher."

"Brother," Mike said, "I wish I was home in bed. If I had a home, and it had a bed."

"I've been in pleasanter spots than this myself. But just remember—if things get sort of vague and bloody, Mike—that all Weber wants is to know where the stuff is."

"Okay. What's the pitch when he comes aboard?"

"We haven't found the *Santa Ybel* yet. We've been looking for it, but we haven't found it yet."

"Why don't you just give him a fake position, Pete? Then he'll go highballing off and leave us alone. Let him kick us around a little and then give him the fake."

Pete looked up slowly at Mike. "Because if he believed us, if he thought he had really beaten the position out of us, there would be no reason for him not to shoot us, sink the *Indra,* and go on about his business. This is a big ocean."

"Oh," Mike said softly.

"That's why we've got to keep it the way it is," Pete said quietly. "As long as Weber doesn't know, he—won't kill us."

Mike nodded slowly. "That sort of stretches out the beating, doesn't it?"

"Yep."

Then a loud, harsh voice floated across the water from the sloop.

"Aho-o-oy, *Indra*."

Pete turned, looked at the man, his face covered by the black ring of the megaphone, and then idly lifted his arm and waved it in answer to the hail.

The voice said, "I would like to come aboard. Will you anchor your ship?"

Pete waved again. "Let her go," he said to Mike.

Mike walked slowly forward, kicked the trigger on the capstan, and the anchor dropped down to the bottom again. He let out scope and then came back to sit down in the cockpit.

Men on the sloop put over a boat, and Pete suddenly grinned. "That's our dinghy."

"One . . . two . . . and Weber makes three," Mike said, counting the men climbing down into the dinghy.

"I don't see but one left aboard the sloop."

"Just one."

The dinghy began to move toward them, the short oars kicking up bright sparkles of spray.

Pete said slowly, "When I was in the Navy, I found that when you're taking a beating you've got to fix your mind on a few simple little thoughts, Mike. If you don't, and the beating is bad, you forget what you're supposed to do. We've got two simple things to remember. First, no matter what happens, we mustn't let our minds go adrift. If we get to the point where we don't know what we're thinking any more, there's no telling what we'll say or do. Second, we —do—not—know—where the *Santa Ybel* is."

"Five by five, Cap'n," Mike said. "Hold your hat."

The Noose Draws Tight

Pete, thinking *This is the enemy, this tall, thin man with eyes as flat and cruel as a snake's*, looked at Weber standing in the cockpit with his two companions. One was a heavy-set, blue-jowled man with no neck between his head and his shoulders, the other a very erect man with a head which looked almost rectangular.

"We meet again, Mr. Martin," Weber said pleasantly.

Pete nodded.

"And you," he said, nodding his long chin at Mike. "Haven't we met before?"

"Not socially," Mike said. "You hit me with a pistol once."

"Oh yes. You are very handy with a marline-spike."

"You're no slouch yourself," Mike said.

Weber turned back to Pete. "I think we can dispense with the preliminaries, Mr. Martin. We haven't much time, and I have already spent five years searching for the Spanish ship."

"Well, if you've found her, we might as well go home."

Weber ignored him. "Shall we go below, Mr. Martin? I do not care for the sunlight."

"You wouldn't," Pete said. He waved his arm toward the companionway. All five of them went below. Pete leaned against the bulkhead; Mike stretched out comfortably on the one remaining bunk and put his hands under his head so that he could see Weber. One of Weber's men stood in the doorway. The other sat down on the gear locker. Weber, in clean white clothes, HW embroidered on the pocket of his shirt, and a yachting cap with a floppy MacArthur top, stood in the middle of the room.

"For five years," Weber said slowly, his voice soft and dreamy, "I have searched. I discovered that Narvez, the elder, possessed the log of the ship. I tried to get it——"

"Narvez told me that," Pete said. "A little business of murder."

Weber's face changed, but for only an instant as an emotion raced across it. "Only a series of accidents."

"Who're you kidding?"

"Yes. However, I failed to get it." He pointed at Pete. "You got it. You and your cute little Navy got it."

Pete nodded.

Weber's whole attitude suddenly changed. He seemed to grow taller, his flat gray eyes began to glitter, his voice sounded like tearing canvas. "*Where is it?*"

"In the post office in a certain town in the United States addressed to a certain man I know," Pete said. "In care of General Delivery."

Weber seemed to relax. His voice got soft again. He began to rock slowly back and forth on his rubber-soled shoes. "You are careful, my friend —and smart. I do not underestimate your ability. Will you give me the same compliment?"

"Sure," Pete said.

"Sure," Mike said. "You're a sharp operator."

Weber bowed elaborately from the waist. "Thank you—both. And now—where is it?"

"Wouldn't you like to search the *Indra,* Weber? Go ahead—open the bilges, search the paneling. You won't find any treasure."

Weber stopped rocking back and forth. "Let us be more serious," he said, his voice very low. "This is a particularly lonely part of the ocean, Mr. Martin. There are no ship lanes in the vicinity, and only wandering fishermen ever come here. . . . You understand, don't you?"

"Oh yes," Pete said. "Perfectly."

"My patience is running out. Five years is a long time. The disappearance of your ship would be a tragedy, especially if she should disappear with you and that little monster aboard her."

"Look who's talking," Mike said, uncrossing and crossing his legs again more comfortably.

Pete straightened a little. "Go back and start that one again."

Weber shrugged. "I don't like to be unpleasant, but I will wait no longer. Tell me where the Spanish ship is or . . . your ship, your friend, and you will all disappear. Is that plain enough?"

"It was okay the first time," Pete said. "Only you left out something."

"I do not agree."

"Oh yeah. You left out the part about the latitude and longitude. If I should accidentally disappear, you couldn't ever find her."

Weber suddenly laughed. "Thank you, my friend. That was what I wanted you to say." He stepped suddenly close to Pete. "So you *do* know where it is."

Pete looked at him, their eyes on a level. "That school Hitler sent you to taught you a lot of tricks, didn't it?"

Weber's eyelids drew a little tighter and then relaxed again. "I am continually being impressed by your thoroughness, Mr. Martin. I congratulate you."

"Skip it," Pete said. "Now listen, flyweight, stop trying to push me around. If I had found the treasure, this ship would be full of it right now, wouldn't it? But—there isn't a dime's worth of stuff aboard her. Where does that leave you? Right where you always were, just a little behind the guy out in front. You won't do any disappearing act with me, Weber, because you know that I can come a lot closer to finding her than you can. And you know that this third-rate Nazi bully-boy business is all a bluff."

Weber suddenly swung his hand and hit Pete across the eyes. Involuntary tears rolled out on Pete's cheeks, and he wiped them away with the tips of his fingers. Mike sat up in the bunk, swinging his feet down to the floor. The man in the doorway stiffened. The other one got up from the gear locker.

"Are you sure that it is a bluff, my friend?" Weber asked. He took out a big white handkerchief and wiped his hand.

Pete let his breath whistle out slowly between his teeth. "Yeah. It's a bluff," he said.

Weber hit him again. Mike jumped from the bunk, but the man grabbed him by the shirt and threw him back again. As Mike came boiling up, Pete said, "Keep your shirt on, Mike, and sit still."

Then Pete turned to Weber. "Okay, knock that off or I'll stop explaining some simple facts to you."

"That was nothing," Weber said.

"Depends on who's taking it. Personally I'm tired of being slapped by that bony thing you call a hand."

Weber stepped close again. Mike looked at the two guards and braced himself to leap.

"I want one thing, Mr. Martin. I will get it. It may mean that I will have to put you through great pain, perhaps even maim and cripple you. But I will get the information."

"Aw, shut up," Pete said. "Try listening. . . . As I explained before—if I knew where it was I would have, by now, *some* of the stuff aboard this ship. Since I haven't got any of it, it should be apparent even to you that I haven't found it. *But* I know her location better than you do, Weber. I can come closer to her than you can. . . . Do you want me to draw you a picture?"

"Please go on with your pretty tale," Weber said.

"Okay. You and your hoodlums start putting

the pressure on me. I can't take it. I give you a latitude and longitude. You follow?"

"My ideas exactly, my friend."

"I thought so," Pete said. "But you keep leaving out stuff. For instance, you beat me up until you break it out of me. How will you know that I gave you the right numbers? This is a big area around here."

"Don't worry, my friend, you will."

"Maybe so. I understand that you Nazis got pretty good at torturing people. But—how will you *know*? While you search mile after mile of bottom, how will you *know* that I gave you the right numbers? One, two, three, four, five, six . . ."

"I warn you, Martin. My patience is ended."

"Forget it. . . . So there's no point in breaking me all up because you'll never know whether I told the truth."

"There is always the little monster," Weber said. "You two will be separated but both will receive a certain amount of—what shall we call it?—the treatment. Both will talk."

"You can do better than that," Pete said. "That's a street urchin I picked up in Miami. Does he look like he can tell north from south, latitude from longitude? Does he just automatically remember ten or twelve numbers in an exact sequence? Just for the fun of it? . . . You can count him out. Stay up in the league with me."

"You are most persuasive," Weber said.

"Thanks. In other words, a great light is beginning to dawn on you, isn't it, pal? Now if I'd found the Spanish ship, it would all be different, wouldn't it? All you'd have to do would be to hammer on me until I talked. And you could check my talk within an hour and, if you found nothing, you could come back and hammer some more. Until at last you did get the right answer. But you see, Weber, there isn't any treasure aboard here, there isn't any trace of evidence that I've found her. So there you are again, up solid against that old 'How do you *know?*' "

Something inside Pete had been lying still, waiting. It was almost as though he had been holding his breath. Now it began to wake up. As he watched Weber walk slowly over and lean against the galley bulkhead, Pete could feel the triumph rising steadily inside him.

The battle was over. And Pete had won. He had planted a seed of doubt in Weber's mind, and it had grown and blossomed into a tangle of briers.

Pete glanced for an instant at Mike and almost imperceptibly winked an eye. Mike let a shadow of a smile flit across his lips.

Pete turned back to Weber. "So, good-by, Weber."

Weber had been leaning with one arm resting on a shelf. As he straightened, he looked at the sleeve of his white shirt, pulling it around on his arm.

There was a smudge of rust on the white silk.

Weber pulled out the handkerchief and began to scrub at the smudge. When he had cleaned it off as much as he could, he turned, frowning, and looked at the shelf.

Pete followed his glance.

Lying on the shelf was the deadeye, covered now with rust so that it looked fuzzy and soft.

A silence as solid as stone filled the cabin and seemed to hold the people in it motionless.

Then Weber moved. Pete saw his bony fingers reaching, saw the white silk shirt sleeve dangling gracefully from the skinny arm. With two fingers, as though the thing was dirty, Weber lifted the deadeye by the rusted metal shank and held it, block downward, so that the wooden insert with the three shroud eyes looked like the upside-down face of a monkey.

Weber spoke in a low voice in German. The man at the door turned and went up the companion ladder. No one else moved.

The man came back in a little while. He walked to the man sitting on the gear locker and held out to him a Walther P-38 pistol. Then he handed to Weber a small coil of thin rope. Finished, he walked back to the door, spun around, and stood squarely in it, a Steyr submachine gun cradled in one crooked elbow.

"Looks like the makin's of a party," Mike said. His voice was faintly husky, and Pete looked over at him.

Weber pointed toward the bunk. "Sit down, Mr. Martin."

Pete walked slowly over and sat down beside Mike.

Weber held up the deadeye, looked at it, and put it back on the shelf. "I am almost sorry that you overlooked this one so small detail," he said. "Frankly, until it stained my sleeve, you were in control of the situation. Now—I am."

"So I've found her," Pete said. "What makes you think I'll tell you where it is?" He knew that

that was weak. But his triumph was gone; now he was desperate.

Weber said something in German. The man put the P-38 down, took the coil of small rope from Weber, and motioned for Pete to hold out his hands, wrists together.

"Tell him to fly a kite with that rope," Mike said.

Pete shook his head. "We've got to go through this, Mike. Might as well get it over before suppertime."

The man bound Pete's wrists very tightly but not painfully. As he turned to bind Mike's, Pete saw that the rope he had used was a loosely laid up affair, gray in color, and soft in texture. Pete had never seen rope like it.

Finished with Mike, the man walked out into the galley and came back with a deep pan full of water.

Pete remembered then and looked up at Weber. "This is a Jap idea," Pete said.

On Guam, Pete had seen Americans who had been Japanese prisoners of war, who had had the rope-and-water treatment. Some of them had had the rope tied around their heads, running between their teeth. When the rope had been soaked with water and drawn tight by it, the men's cheeks had been split open back to the jawbone.

Weber nodded. "Yes, an idea of our allies. I saw men with their hands paralyzed. Some were even cut off by the little ropes. The Japanese are very clever people."

"What's left of 'em," Pete said. "And I saw Nazis down on their knees begging for mercy, Weber."

"Did you?" Weber asked. Then he slapped Pete, slowly, five times.

When Pete was sure he could talk, he turned to Mike. "Remember those two simple things, Mike," he said.

"Brother, that's all I'm doing," Mike said.

Pete grinned and nodded.

Pete's mind swam out of a haze which seemed to be the color of a thin mixture of yellow mustard and red catsup. Like a man drowning, he fought to keep his mind from sinking back into the haze.

Two simple things. No, for him there were three simple things. What were they? Two simple things. What? He had forgotten them.

The haze came rolling in like a fog, and he fought harder and harder. The pain coming up from the thin, wet rope was constant, and it had been going on so long now that it had killed every other feeling in his body and had pushed everything away until he was full of pain everywhere. The smashing blows which came occasionally seemed, for a moment, to relieve the pain of the rope but after them the haze would darken, the pink color growing steadily deeper.

How many things did he have to remember? Two? Three? Pete fought against a new feeling—nausea. Suddenly he remembered one of the things. "I do not know where the ship is." He did not know whether he said it out loud or not.

That was one of the things. "I do not know where the ship is." But there were some more things. Mike had only two things to remember but he, Pete Martin, had three things.

Oh. He must not let his mind go adrift. He must keep this haze away. There was a feeling in him of sleepiness. Not a good feeling. It was a heavy, drugged feeling. He *must* go to sleep. That was the second thing. He must *not* go to sleep.

What was the other thing? The third thing?

There was a voice somewhere saying over and over again, "Where is it?" Each time the voice said that something would hit him and there would be an explosion inside the haze. It was sort of like lightning flashing behind high, dark clouds. He kept waiting to hear the voice say, "Where is it?" and that made it a lot harder to think about that third thing.

Then he remembered. He had to know what time it was. That was all. Just what time it was.

Pete raised his head a little and opened his eyes. He was surprised to find that he was lying down on the floor, his knees drawn up, his manacled hands up around his head.

All he could see were two vague white blotches which must be Weber's legs, and then shadowy things.

When had he last heard the clock?

It had been a long time ago, he remembered. Five bells. Five bells in the afternoon watch. The navigator would be getting ready to take the 1600 line; the engineering officer would be pulling burners for the evening watch. On deck the gunnery officer would be squaring away after GQ. It was time for java on the bridge. But it was a long time before the boatswain would begin the shrill piping and the loudspeaker would grumble, "Reee-lieeeeve the watch."

But what time was it *now*? How long had this pain lasted? Had six bells struck?

Pete could not remember. He could not hold back the haze any longer. It was sliding in over him so fast, so fast. He was disappearing into it, drowning in it. He couldn't think any more— one thing, two things, three . . .

After what seemed an eternity of slow time Pete struggled up again from the haze. The explosions of pain had stopped, and there was only the stuff coming up from the rope. The voice had stopped saying, "Where is it?"

What had happened? Pete wondered. Was Weber gone? Had he told him? In the haze, while he was down under it, *had he told him?* Pete struggled to lift his head, to open his eyes.

Then he heard a voice. A very clear, familiar voice close to him.

"Hey, you, you punk," the voice said.

It was Mike. Pete slumped back, listening.

Then Mike said, "Yeah, you, Weber. You're not getting anywhere with him. Why don't you pick on somebody your size? Why don't you see if you can make me tell you? Because I know where she is. I know all about it. I memorized the position of it."

Then Weber said, "Oh, did you?"

The haze was slowly drifting away. It seemed to Pete that it wasn't so thick, so dark and red.

"Sure," Mike said.

"Then where is it?"

Pete heard the familiar words and waited for the explosion to burst dirtily inside the haze. But nothing happened.

"Yak, yak," Mike said.

Something white moved past Pete's face, and then Weber said, "Do you want some of what he had?"

"Yeh, try some on—just for size," Mike said.

Pete heard the blow, heard Mike grunt. He tried to move and got his arms down a little. But when he pressed them against the floor, the pain almost crushed him. He tried then to say something, but his tongue was swollen and clotted inside his mouth.

"That was all right," Mike said. "You don't mind if I spit teeth on the deck, do you, jughead?"

"You're wasting time, hurting yourself," Weber said. "Tell me where it is."

"I could remember better without this rope," Mike said. "You know, there're a lot of numbers and stuff."

Weber said something in German and then asked, "Feel better?"

"Much. You ought to try that sometime."

"*Where is it?*"

"In the itty bitty poo, with three little fishes," Mike said.

The haze was dim now and far away. Pete could see all the way across the cabin floor. He could see the spread-apart legs of the man with the burp gun, see the gear locker, the galley door. His mind was clearing fast.

He had been so close to going under—until Mike had drawn Weber away.

Mike was taking the beating now. Pete could hear it. Then something heavy and dead limp fell down on him and rolled slowly off. Pete forced his eyes open again and saw one arm, brown and lined with muscles, and then a grotesquely swollen hand. The whole hand was a deep purple color.

Then the clock in the companionway struck. Pete counted the tinkling bell. . . . Three-four . . . five-six. Pete stopped at six but the bell rang once more.

Seven bells? Pete forced himself to hear them again like an echo. Three-four . . . five-six . . . seven.

I must have missed six bells, Pete thought. They must have come when the haze was down on me.

Pete felt the thing crush against his ribs, felt the new pain. He saw the haze moving slowly toward him again. Then, lying there, he fought against it with all his strength.

He knew only that he *must* not go under again. No matter what Weber did, he must not let the haze roll over him, drown him.

Pete turned slowly over on his back. Straining, the back of his tongue pushing, he at last got the word out of his mashed mouth.

"Enough."

Then something came down on his face, across his mouth. Pete turned his head slowly. Mike was half sitting up, his hand down on Pete's mouth.

"Keep your yap shut, Mac," Mike said.

Pete shook his head from side to side, Mike's helpless hand grinding back and forth across his mouth. At last Pete raised his arms and pushed Mike's arm away.

"Topside," he said to Weber. "Chart."

"Pete," Mike said. "Be quiet. You can take some more, Skipper."

Pete doggedly shook his head.

"Sure you can. He can't hurt you any more, Cap'n. All the rest is just coasting."

Then something white swooped down, and Pete saw Mike reel backward and fall against the drawer faces built under the bunk.

Gentle hands helped Pete up, guided him toward the companionway. They stopped there, and the two men got Mike and brought him, kicking and fighting, up beside Pete.

Mike looked at Pete with his eyes hard and glittery. "Are you going to tell him?"

Pete nodded.

"You lousy punk," Mike said between his teeth.

Pushing Mike up the ladder first, Weber followed with Pete. Halfway up, Pete stopped and wordlessly held out his bound wrists.

"Sorry, my friend," Weber said, and got a gold penknife to cut the rope.

Pete's helpless hands dropped to his sides, and he went on up the ladder, stumbling at each step. At the top, as he stepped down into the cockpit, he swayed sideways. His shoulder swung against the downhaul of the flag hoist and he let his body fall against it until Weber grabbed him and held him upright again.

Faintly, coming down through the taut rope,

Pete had felt small loops of twine snapping under the strain of his weight against them.

Pete licked the blood on his lips. "Water," he said.

Weber snapped an order. One man went below and came up with a pitcher of water. Pete drank it in gulps and then held it out toward Mike, holding the pitcher between his forearms, his swollen and purple hands useless.

"Go drown yourself," Mike said.

Pete lifted the pitcher, trying to pour the water on his head, but the pitcher slipped and fell.

"Are you stalling?" Weber asked.

Pete shook his head. "Sick," he said. "Wait."

"I will wait only one minute," Weber said, glancing at a wrist watch.

Pete nodded. He leaned back against the companion door, his back against the downhaul. A wind was blowing, rippling the blue Gulf, and he could feel the rope fluttering in it.

"Talk," Weber said.

"Bearings," Pete said. "Two islands." He fumbled with his hands at the knob of the chart case. Weber pushed his hands away and pulled out the chart.

"Which ones?" Weber asked. His voice was excited now and trembling and his eyes were bright. They looked like the eyes of that sea gull, Pete thought. Mean and hard.

Pete put his swollen finger down on the first island.

Then Mike suddenly wrenched himself away from the two men and began hitting Pete on the back with his purple hands. Weber shouted in German; the men clubbed Mike to the deck.

"What is the bearing?" Weber asked.

Then Pete heard it. Faint and far away. But he had heard it so many times before. He had heard it at midnight and at dawn and at high noon. The pulsing of it, the imperative beating of it. So he heard it now.

And no one else did.

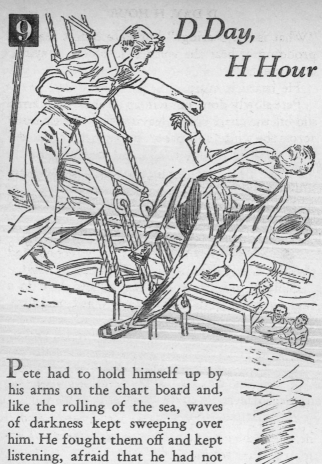

9 D Day, H Hour

Pete had to hold himself up by his arms on the chart board and, like the rolling of the sea, waves of darkness kept sweeping over him. He fought them off and kept listening, afraid that he had not heard it after all. Afraid that he had wanted so much to hear it that his mind had tricked him.

Weber prodded him, saying,

"What is the bearing?" but Pete didn't feel the prodding or hear the voice as he stood, swaying, and listened.

He heard it again.

Pete slowly drew himself up straight. His arms slid off the chart board, leaving two bloody trails across the white, stiff paper. He turned very slowly so that he would not fall and faced Weber.

"That's all," Pete said, his voice so low that Mike hardly heard him.

"What do you mean?" Weber came close to him, the gray eyes narrowing.

"Look aloft, Weber," Pete said.

Weber's flat eyes held Pete's for a second, and then he slowly lifted them and looked upward.

Gaily fluttering in the breeze and held in a taut arc by the flag hoist were pennants and flags. They were brand new, the colors vivid in the sunshine. At the top was the United States ensign. The Stars and Stripes were upside down—the signal of distress. Below it were the other code flags which Pete had wrapped into a bundle, tied with light twine, and hoisted aloft.

Weber's eyes came back to his. "Very pretty," he said. Then he started snapping orders in German to the two men.

In the middle of a sentence one of the men stiffened and cried out, "*Achtung! Achtung!*" Then he pointed.

The blue, sparkling water was being sliced

open in a wide, foaming, white V. Where it curled up forward it was still blue and so smooth that it looked like cut glass. Then it hissed over and flowed downward along the sleek steel hull and boiled out into the V as the wake current poured up into the hull wash.

Pete turned also and looked. He had always thought that the cans were the prettiest things afloat, and as he looked at this one, tears began to burn in his eyes.

From the destroyer escort the last notes of the bugle, the last clanging of the gongs died and the ship stood at General Quarters. With the men at their battle stations, all guns manned, the torpedo tubes swung outboard, the DE didn't take off a knot as it swept down on the anchored *Indra* and the black sloop to port of her.

Pete heard the order to the helmsman—"Put her hard over"—and he watched the DE heel until her scupper was almost awash and then come up again, all engines going astern. She slid smoothly alongside the *Indra* and Wild Bill Williams's familiar voice called, "Hiya, Pete? What's cookin'?"

"Can you come aboard?" Pete called.

"Be right with you."

Weber said something in German, and one of the men turned Mike loose and began to untie the the painter of the dinghy. The other man cradled the burp under his arm and handed Weber the P-38.

Weber held the pistol down low, close to Pete's stomach. "We are going now," he said in a low voice. "Tell your friend to let us go without any trouble, Martin, or I will shoot you and the kid. I mean this."

And then Bill's pleasant, slow voice from the DE towering above the *Indra* said, "Tell that skinny guy to put away the gun. Before I drop something on him."

Weber looked up toward the side of the DE. He looked straight into the muzzle of a machine gun. A sailor, stripped to the waist, was looking down at Weber through the ring sight.

Weber put the P-38 on the bloody chart and stepped back. He was smiling a little as he said, "Now we must go through this all over again."

Pete shook his head. "This fixes your clock, Weber."

"No. The Spanish ship is still there, my friend."

"That's right," Pete said, "but there's nothing in her—now."

"I will be waiting for you to come back."

"Why not come along with me?"

Then Williams swarmed up the side of the *Indra*. Under the salty cap he was wearing his face had a set, hard expression. Pete had seen it before on that day when Wild Bill had helped fire the last shot from the sinking *Hoel*. He looked slowly around the cockpit and then turned to Pete.

"What kind of party is this? Hiya, Pete. What's been going on? Who's the little squirt?" he asked, glancing at Mike.

"Look who's talking," Mike said.

"I got your SOS and I thought you were kidding, but I didn't have anything else to do so I slid on down here. But it doesn't look much like kidding, does it? . . . So you're Weber? . . . What's he done to your hands, Pete? And the squirt's? Saaa-ay, what goes on around here, anyway?" he demanded of Weber.

"Yeah," Pete said, out of his broken mouth, "this is Weber. A very nosy character. And he plays—rough."

Bill turned and looked Weber up and down. "You been kicking my pal around?" he asked slowly.

"I am a citizen of the United States," Weber said.

"Good. The authorities frown on us beating up our late enemies." Williams stooped and picked up the bloody rope which had bound Pete's wrists. He looked at it, dropped it, and looked at Pete's helpless hands.

"Been up to dirty work, haven't you?" he demanded of Weber. "Japoon stuff. . . . Pete, I hate to deprive you of the pleasure but I am going to place my fist upon your friend."

"Help yourself," Pete said.

"One for me," Mike said.

"Are you not an officer in the Navy?" Weber asked.

"Sure am. And I'm going to be mighty undignified in about a minute." Williams unpinned the tarnished gold oak leaves from the tabs of his shirt. He took off the beat-up, salty cap and then took off the heavy Annapolis ring. Then he held his forefinger under Weber's nose and crooked it.

"Come along," he said. "And take off that fancy hat."

Weber shook his head.

Williams snapped, "Get forward or I'll beat you down right in front of your friends." Then he pushed Weber with his open hand.

Weber struck with the speed of a snake. Blood spurted out of Wild Bill's nose as he crashed back against the wheelbox.

An angry muttering came down from the men lining the rail of the DE.

Williams scooped the blood off with his hand and straightened.

Mike said, "Hit him again, shorty—with your nose."

Williams grinned at Mike. Then he leaped without, apparently, looking at Weber. Pete backed out of the way and shoved the chart board into the case.

Wild Bill beat Weber up out of the cockpit, aft along the narrow walk, and at last knocked him under the gallows frame and into the water. Then he pulled a huge red handkerchief out of his hip pocket and wiped his nose.

"Fish him out," he said to the crew of the lifeboat.

On the DE there was a low, dignified cheer.

"Now, Pete," Bill said, putting his cap back on, "let's get you and the mighty midget into sick bay. You look pretty beat up. And then tell me all about it."

Pete shook his head. "Can you talk to FBI in Miami?"

"Boy, I got a new juke box aboard that can talk to anybody. But don't worry about Skinny there. I'll take care of him."

"I refuse to go aboard your ship," Weber said.

"Listen to him!" Bill snorted. "Get aboard. You're a sick man. My first duty is to save your ugly life."

"This is against international law," Weber said. "I will report you."

"Aw, shut up," Williams said.

Aboard the DE Pete, Mike, and Wild Bill sat in the captain's cabin. Pete and Mike had rolls of white bandage from shoulder to finger tips.

"Let's get everything squared away, Pete. First, we'll dig up that gold out of the lagoon. You're not kidding me about that, are you? Next, if the FBI wants Weber, we'll tow that black job to Miami. Third, we'll leave the *Indra* here and you can send down for her. Fourth, if nobody wants Weber, we'll leave him here. Is that right?"

Pete nodded.

Williams started to say something when the communications officer came in. "FBI doesn't want him," the officer said, "but the Treasury boys do. Apparently he owes Uncle Sam a wad of cabbage."

"Do they want me to bring him?"

"If you please, Captain."

"Okay. Let's go get that cockeyed calendar, Pete."

The DE was sliding toward Miami, the black sloop being towed astern by a thousand-foot wire. Williams had taken the dinghy away from Weber and had posted a man astern on the DE to report if anybody went overboard and tried to swim for it. The main searchlight battery was trained aft to floodlight the sloop during the night run.

Pete and Williams on the bridge watched the mast of the sloop waving. "Stop worrying about your skinny chum," Williams said. "He's not going to jump overboard because we're not going to be within fifty miles of land for a long time. When we get up close to Florida, I'll take him aboard. But I don't want him stinking up my ship any longer than necessary."

Pete looked down on the main deck. In an area marked off by ropes were the dripping, sandy, ugly crates and boxes with the golden Wheel of Years piled on top. A sailor with a carbine walked slowly around and around the ropes. Occasionally a working party under an old chief petty officer would come topside, pick up one of the crates, and carry it below to the metalsmith's shop.

"Where was the *Santa Ybel*, Pete?"

Pete glanced across the compass at the two islands fading astern. "Right about here, Bill. And she isn't 'was.' She's still down there."

"Let's go below and see what the metalsmith has got to say. I'll bet you a duck dinner it isn't gold."

Pete held out his bandaged hand. "I'll take that."

In the metalsmith's shop the old chief turned around as Williams' and Pete came in. "Captain," he said, "did you ever see anything as pretty?" Then he picked up a life-sized statue of a hummingbird. In the hard electric light it shone warm and polished.

"See the feathers marked out and the little beak?" the chief said. "There's a whole box full of nothing but birds and we haven't found any two of 'em alike." He pointed to a shelf lined with big and little golden birds.

"What are they made out of, Chief?" Williams asked.

"Captain, they ain't brass."

"Tell me right, Chief. I've got a duck dinner up that it isn't gold."

The chief grinned at Pete. "I hope you enjoy the dinner. The captain doesn't give 'em away very often."

Pete picked up the little hummingbird between his two bandaged paws. "Here," he said, holding it out toward Williams.

Wild Bill stared at him.

"Here!" Pete said. "Before I drop it."

Williams cupped his hands.

"Take it. Your dad won't need 'em all. By the way, have you heard anything from him?"

"I forgot. He sent a message saying he and the staffs from six museums and the aquarium would be waiting on the dock."

"They'd better have a pocketful of money," Pete said. "Mike wants a red bicycle."

"What a character!" Williams said, laughing. "I'll bet he's down in the CPO mess right now."

That's where Mike was, with three chiefs helping him eat a lobster dinner while he entertained them with the story of the *Santa Ybel*.

"When you get through, you might wander aft to the metalsmith's shop and take a look, Mike," Pete said.

"I showed 'em how to clean the stuff," Mike

said. "Boy, aren't those little birds pretty? How's about me keeping one of 'em, Mac?" Mike thanked the chief petty officers and went with Pete as he and Williams started topside.

"Take your choice," Pete said. "They're as much yours as mine."

"Think of all the people who'll come to look at 'em in the museum, Pete. You guess they'll know how they got in there?"

"Sure. We'll make the museum put up a sign. 'Found by Mike——' What's your last name, anyway?"

"What's it to you, Mac?" Mike asked. For a moment he glared at Pete, then he looked away. "Never had any. Not that I know of," he said softly.

"Try 'Martin.' Just for size," Pete said.

They were almost topside when the explosion came. The shock of it threw Pete heavily against the bulkhead, hurting his arm, and then they heard the dull ca-rump and the echoing roar.

Williams went up the ladder three at a time and burst out on deck. People were getting to their feet again, one man was groaning in the scupper with a nasty cut on his head, the sentry was looking for his carbine.

Aft the tow wire, frayed into a whisk broom at the end, snaked back and forth in the water.

The black sloop was gone. Where it had been there were splinters of it floating and a sail, gray

316

with water, slowly sank. A ring of oil began to spread, iridescent in the sunlight.

Williams climbed to the bridge with Pete behind him.

"Get the wire in. . . . Hard left rudder. . . . Stand by the starboard lifeboat." Then Williams looked at Pete.

The DE circled the growing ring of oil and at last cut through it. There was nothing left of the sloop bigger than the blade of an oar.

"Weber must have been scared to death of the people in Miami waiting for him," Pete said.

"They must have wanted him for more than income tax."

Pete nodded. "When I first asked about him, I got a very guarded answer from ONI."

"Well . . . Put her back on course. . . . Secure on the lifeboat. . . . All engines ahead standard. . . . Quartermaster, enter, 'Tow exploded at 2011. Cause of explosion unknown. No personnel recovered. Tow wire reeled in. Search thorough and complete. Missing: Herman Weber, NOK and address unknown. Two others, male, adult, identity unknown.' "

Then he and Pete turned to the windows of the bridge and watched the sea grow dark as night came in.

No Bright Red Bicycle

Pete, his bandages not so conspicuous under the sleeves of his coat, waited in the hot sunshine for Mike, and when at last he came, Pete said, "You could have bought a dozen bicycles. What've you been doing?"

Mike was scowling. "The lunkhead said he didn't have any red bicycles. He didn't have any bicycles at all. He said maybe he could get me a tricycle, the meathead. . . . Where's the bus?"

Pete pointed up the empty street and then looked at Mike. He looked all right, Pete decided. He had on shoes and there was some evidence of a crease left in his pants and his shirt was clean, although the combination of red, green, and purple squares wasn't what Pete would have picked out.

The bus came and they got aboard, finding a seat together in the back. Mike looked gloomily out the window, and as the bus left Miami and began to hurtle along, Mike pulled an immense roll of money out of his pants pocket and looked at it scornfully.

"What good is it? There isn't a bicycle for sale. Think I'll throw it out the window."

"Go ahead," Pete said.

Mike grinned and put the money back in his pocket. "How're your hands?"

"Coming along."

"Mine are about well. But I didn't have what Weber called the 'treatment' as long as you did. . . . Boy, those museum people! I thought they were going to get in a fight right on the dock."

"Did you see the one with the beard when he looked at the Wheel? I thought he was going over backwards in a dead faint."

"I thought his eyes were going to jump out and roll on the deck. . . . How far we got to go?"

"Not far."

"They got anything to eat in this hospital?"

"Crackers and milk."

"Crackers and milk, he says. Well, you talk to your kid brother, and I bet I can rustle up a steak."

"You get tough and they'll throw you out."

"Who, me? Listen, Mac, they get tough with me and . . . I'll buy the joint."

Pete grinned and looked past Mike at the green orchards. Mike turned also. For a while they both watched the fields and trees sweeping past.

"Nice day to be running around," Mike said at last. "Wonder if Johnny can do any better than wiggle his right thumb? We've been gone a long time."

"It takes a long time," Pete said.

"It's a funny thing," Mike said slowly. "We got all the money in the world, and it doesn't do a bit of good. I can't get a red bicycle, and Johnny can't ride one."

The bus sighed to a stop outside the high walls with the ivy growing on them. As Mike walked beside Pete to the gates, he said, "I still haven't got my shore legs yet. The ground keeps going up and down. Last night that hotel bed nearly tossed me out on the deck."

"Me, too," Pete said.

Pete was glad the place didn't smell like a hospital. There were some cape jasmine bushes around the front, and everything smelled faintly of jasmine.

The man said Johnny was around back, and Pete and Mike walked along a gravel path. Behind the hospital there was a broad lawn with trees growing in it and at the edge a little crooked stream. Out in the middle of the lawn was a wheel chair and a nurse in a white dress was sitting on the grass beside it.

Mike whispered, "Is that him, Cap'n?"

Pete nodded.

"I think I'll just wait around here," Mike said, still whispering. "I'll mess around here a while."

"Okay."

Pete walked slowly across the clipped, thick grass. The nurse saw him coming and got up. As he got closer, she turned the chair around.

Johnny saw him and began to grin. Then the nurse slipped two crutches under his arms and, very slowly, Johnny raised himself. The nurse helped him when he swayed, but at last he stood straight up on the crutches. Then he began to grin again.

Pete's throat was so tight he was afraid he wouldn't be able to talk.

He stopped walking a few feet from Johnny. " 'Lo," he said.

" 'Lo, Pete."

"How are you, Jawn?"

"Good. Say, you look a little wrung out."

"I'm okay, Jawn . . ."

The nurse went away, her dress rustling a little. She walked over to where Mike was leaning against a tree, his back to Pete and Johnny.

"Good morning," the nurse said.

"How you do?" Mike said.

"That's Johnny's brother, isn't it?"

"Yeh. His name's Pete. Pete Martin. My name's Martin, too. Mike Martin."

"Oh, are you kin to Johnny?"

Mike looked at her and then looked up into the sky. "In a way," he said.

"Johnny's a grand boy."

"So's Pete."

"I never saw anyone with so much courage," the nurse said.

"Me neither."

"Who?"

"Pete."

"No, I meant Johnny."

"Well, lady," Mike said, "I meant Pete."

The nurse smiled. "You think a lot of Pete, don't you?"

"Why not? Listen, lady, if Johnny is half the man Pete is, then he's okay, see?"

"I see," the nurse said. "Well, he is. Why don't you go over and talk to him?"

"Oh . . . well. Naw, I can't. I told Pete I'd get us something to eat."

322

"No. You go talk to Johnny, and I'll get something to eat. What would you like?"

"Oh, just a little something."

"Steak . . . French fries . . . onions?"

Mike grinned. "I bet you do all right as a nurse."

"Maybe. You go talk to Johnny."

Pete was calling him, and Mike went slowly over. He looked at Johnny for a while and then said, "You're doing all right. We thought you were lying up in a sack."

Johnny grinned. "I can even walk . . . a little."

"Take it easy, kid," Mike said. "We're going to get you out of here in a little while. Aren't we, Pete?"

Pete grinned and nodded.

Mike shuffled his feet around and then pulled a lump out of his pocket. It was wrapped in brown grocery paper. "I brought you something to fool around with," he said. He held it out, then drew it back. "Say, I forgot. You're about in the same shape as Pete."

Mike tore the wrapping paper off and held out one of the golden birds. "That's what Pete dug up," he said.

Pete started to say something, and Mike scowled at him. "What do I want with a little gold bird?" he demanded. "Can't fly. Can't holler. Can't even lay an egg. Here."

Johnny balanced himself carefully and then

held out one hand. Mike put the bird in it and wrapped Johnny's fingers around it. "You can throw it at the nurse if she bothers you," Mike said.

"Thanks, Mike," Johnny said. "Let me sit down and then tell me what happened."

Pete, with Mike supplying any details he left out, was halfway through the story when the nurse came back. Behind her was another girl who was pushing a rubber-wheeled truck with rows of shiny pots lined up on it.

The two nurses began setting plates and opening the pots. The steaks were sizzling on the platters they had been cooked on, and steam came up from the onions.

"Boy!" Mike said. "Now this is my idea of a picnic. No ants."

They finished telling Johnny the story as they ate, and after Mike had wiped his plate clean with a piece of bread, he leaned back on his elbows, a blade of grass between his teeth.

"Wonder what the old *Santa Ybel* is doing now?" Mike asked.

"Don't know. But Weber blew his sloop up very close to where she was. Might have rattled her," Pete said.

Mike said softly, "I hope not."

But the explosion of the *Auf Wiedersehen* had

done more than that. As the concussion of it packed downward a crab had stopped moving. A purple pecten close beside the *Santa Ybel* slowly closed its fluted shells as the shock struck it. Fish near the surface turned belly up and some of them never recovered.

The wave of shock died as it moved away from the blasted sloop but there was still enough power in it to make the *Santa Ybel* tremble. This trembling loosened grains of sand and they slipped, pushing other grains. A little running cloud of wet dust rose along the southern side of the *Santa Ybel*. More sand slipped. Things alive scuttled away from the ship as she moved, slowly at first, and then fast, tumbling down and down into the thousand-foot deep.

She struck bottom at last and lay, finally broken, beside the shattered Nazi submarine.